The
PLASTIC
Priest

Cemetery Dance Publications
132B Industry Lane, Unit #7
Forest Hill, MD 21050

www.cemeterydance.com

The
PLASTIC
Priest

NICOLE CUSHING

The Childless Mother Introduced

Reverend Ford is not Reverend Ford. At least, not to her parishioners. To them, she's "Mother Kaye."

"Mother" because it has long been customary for Episcopalians to call their male priests "Father", like the Catholics. "Kaye" because she goes by her middle name.

Kaye is actually an old family surname, her great-grandmother's maiden name. It was never intended to be a first name. Mother Kaye's full, legal name is Heather Kaye Ford. She started going by Kaye in college. She was tired of everyone making jokes about her name. (The movie *Heathers* came out in her sophomore year of high school.)

Her maiden name was Martin. Heather Martin became Kaye Martin in college. She became Reverend Kaye upon ordination. She became Kaye Ford after she got married. She became Mother Kaye shortly after her arrival at her first church.

Her parishioners always misspell it ("Mother Kay"). A well-to-do octogenarian widow at St. Luke's calls her "Mary Kay". Mother Kaye never corrects her. Doing so might alienate her. The widow's checks never bounce, and the church needs money.

Mother Kaye hates to think of her parishioners as bipedal checkbooks, but it's difficult to avoid. She wants to keep the doors open, so a kinder, gentler version of Christianity has a platform in this harsh, crass town. A liberal version, to be honest, that offers an alternative to the Republican talking points preached from other pulpits.

Also, she wants to keep her job.

Mother Kaye has considered the merits of simply going by "Mother K". She has always balked, though. It would be too Kafkaesque. Very few of her parishioners would think it was Kafkaesque. They've probably never learned about Kafka. They wouldn't get the reference. Nevertheless, *she* would get the reference and that would be unpleasant.

Once upon a time, only men were allowed to be Episcopal priests. That changed in the seventies. Mother Kaye was born in 1973. She was ordained in 1999. She married a pagan high school teacher named Charlie Ford in 2003. They met on eharmony. They both enjoy cats, books, and hiking.

This might not seem like a sufficiently strong foundation for a marriage, but it is. At least, *in rural Indiana*, it is. Here, dogs are more loved than cats. Guns are more loved than books. Hunting is more loved than hiking. Perhaps this explains why Kaye and Charlie overlooked their religious differences. And in case you find all of these reasons lacking, consider this: neither wanted children.

The algorithm knew what it was doing.

Charlie is the more attractive of the two. Kaye considers herself lucky to have snagged him. He shows up to church services about half the time. He understands the need to keep up appearances, but he can only stomach so much. He practices his true faith in secret, tramping off to drum circles and sweat lodges and paranormal conventions in nearby cities. (Indianapolis, Chicago, Louisville, Cincinnati, Columbus, etc.)

The congregation at St. Luke's isn't ready for Charlie to come out as pagan. They had a hard enough time just accepting Mother Kaye into their midst. They'd idolized her predecessor, a skinny, bespectacled, half-bald old man named Father Abbott. He'd served St. Luke's for nearly twenty years, and never wore out his welcome.

Wilmore Abbott, that was his full name. The parishioners who came from old money got to call him "Willy", because he'd come from old money himself (Dartmouth '59) and most rich people only consider other rich people their equals. The middle class parishioners loved him, too, though. They loved him for his sermons (orthodox, confident) and his charm (genteel, tireless). When he was the priest, St. Luke's averaged around one hundred and fifty congregants per week.

But attrition has taken its toll. For the last five years, the average Sunday attendance has consistently hovered around twenty-five. When Father Abbott died, nobody could fill his shoes. When the diocese sent Mother Kaye to replace him, the congregation didn't warm up. She was socially awkward. She was a woman. Thus, in small town Indiana, she started out with two strikes against her.

Charlie coming out as pagan would be strike three. So, he hides his tarot cards and Pan figurines in his underwear drawer. (You never know when church people will come to visit.) Kaye knows he resents this, but he never complains.

Unlike their Catholic counterparts, Episcopal priests have always been allowed to marry. It's not unusual to see them wearing black shirts and black slacks and white clerical collars (like the Catholics) along with wedding rings (like the Protestants). Father Abbott always confused the town gossips. Why was a Catholic priest taking a woman out to dinner? ("At least he's not diddling altar boys," they whispered.)

No amount of explanation can correct the misunderstanding. For example: at an interfaith dinner, an Episcopalian can try to explain the history, traditions, and clergy of their church to a Methodist and the latter will nod and seem to understand. Then, a week later, the Methodist will be gossiping about Mother Kaye ("...that nun who runs around with a man").

Is the Methodist intentionally distorting the facts? No. They've honestly forgotten everything the Episcopalian told them the week before. The information was too nuanced and obscure to stick.

Obscure? Is that a valid adjective? Some would argue the Episcopal Church is far from obscure. After all, eleven U.S. presidents were Episcopalian!

True, but most of them held office during the nineteenth century. The most recent was George H.W. Bush. It's worth noting, however, that his son George W. left the Episcopal Church to become a Methodist, and that there seems to be no hint of him (or any other notable politician) returning to the Anglican tradition.

Time marches on.

The Episcopal Church is the American outgrowth of the Church of England. It does best on the Eastern Seaboard, in the erstwhile colonies, where it has the advantage of hereditary transmission. Southern Indiana, on the other hand, was settled by the Scots Irish. Here, the Presbyterians and Southern Baptists and Pentecostals and Methodists and "non-denominational" fundamentalist megachurches dominate the market. The town doesn't quite know what to do with its Episcopalians.

Mother Kaye doesn't quite know what to do with the town. The Diocese wants her to get young families in the door, but the Episcopal Church's brand doesn't mesh with what young Midwestern families expect. The Episcopal Church, at its best, is cool, calm, and collected. It rests on a three-legged stool of scripture, tradition, and reason.

These days, most of its priests don't take the Bible literally. If Mother Kaye were being fully transparent with her congregation, she'd tell them she doesn't believe in miracles. She'd confess she thinks they're myths. Not myths as in "trite fairy tales", but myths in the Joseph Campbell sense of the word: deep stories that define the human condition.

Mother Kaye never confesses her true beliefs. She wouldn't want to upset the unity of the faith community. Publicly aligning with any particular interpretation of scripture would leave members who disagreed with her feeling left out. She has a responsibility to be a shepherd to *all* of her flock.

Also, she wants to keep her job.

But *can* she keep her job? How can she possibly succeed? Episcopalians aren't driven by frothy emotionalism, and we live in an era *defined* by frothy emotionalism. Congregants in the Episcopal Church feel the *subtle warm glow* of God's presence. Subtle, but steady. Episcopalians don't often experience harsh peaks and valleys in their spiritual walk. If they get fired up by anything, it's politics. Faith, not so much.

That said, Mother Kaye tries to avoid too much conversation about social justice. If she were in Indianapolis or Louisville things might be different, but she's in a small town. Her congregation would soon grow weary of sermons about Fixing the World.

"Grow weary" is exactly the right phrase, too. Most Sundays, her congregation is populated by the retired, the soon-to-be-retired, and seniors who can't afford to retire. They haven't much interest in Fixing the World. They're close to death and want the assurance of eternal life in Heaven.

Mother Kaye believes in the promise of eternal life. At least, *most of the time* she believes. However, her mental picture of Heaven departs from tradition: it borrows nothing from Dante's *Paradiso*, nor does it look anything like the Heaven depicted by Renaissance painters. No pageantry. No clouds. No robes. No chanting angels. No halos.

She finds such images hackneyed and melodramatic. She dislikes their grandeur. When she goes to Heaven, she'd prefer to dwell in the *subtle warm glow* of God's presence.

Maybe it will be like an eternally pleasant family picnic, held on an eternally pleasant spring day, interrupted only by pleasant naps. The children will never scream too much or too loudly. No one will have to go to the bathroom. No one will say anything objectionable. Everyone will talk *of love*, and about *the things they love*, and they'll be out in the sun *doing what they love*.

But they won't *make love*. At least, not out in public. They'll go off into their own separate cabins to do that. Then they'll shower and hang out in hot tubs. Then they'll play volleyball.

It will be an intergenerational game; grandparents, parents, and children all playing with equal fervor. They'll keep volleys going for minutes at a time. Everyone will be diving and lunging after the ball. Everyone will hit the ball over the net. Well, almost everyone. The children and elderly will fuck up, from time to time. But they'll do so in an entertaining way. Thus, points will be scored, but no one will bother keeping track of them.

Once, Mother Kaye invoked this simile in her sermon. "Maybe it will be like an eternally pleasant family picnic," she said. She ended with the image of the volleyball game, and with a line she thought particularly poignant: "Heaven is a place where no one keeps score."

No one in the congregation openly criticized her after that sermon, but their sour expressions betrayed their disappointment. In retrospect, she realized they'd expected something loftier than a picnic and volleyball game. Besides, people don't want to be told they'll have to exercise in Heaven.

Being a priest is a thankless job. Mother Kaye knows, in the back of her mind, that she'll never be able to grow her congregation. So the Bishop will never be pleased with her. Mother Kaye is required to work weekends. So her husband will never be pleased with her. She has little in common with her flock. She would not voluntarily spend time with any of them and the feeling is mutual. They are a dull, entitled, weak-minded bunch who hate her for the same reason they hate all outsiders and "transplants". So the congregation will never be pleased with her. Congregations have *never* been pleased with her. She has served seven during her career. Some have been slightly less dull, entitled, and weak-minded.

But only slightly.

Despite all these frustrations, the question "Why do I keep doing this?" seldom enters her mind. It's an unwelcome question. When it knocks on the door she shoos it away. *We*, however, have the freedom to look at certain matters Mother Kaye would rather avoid. So, let's fling open the door of her head and crack open the vault of her heart. Let's find out why she continues going through the motions of being a priest.

Seven Reasons Kaye Doesn't Change Careers

1. Middle age inertia.

Mother Kaye is forty-seven years old. If she plays her cards right, she might be able to retire at age sixty-two. She has already been a priest for twenty years. What's another fifteen? The salary isn't bad, all things considered. The benefits are solid. She gets to take off a lot of time in August. The Church supplies her with a substitute for the whole month!

If she switched to another field, it would be counseling. Then she wouldn't have to tell people what Heaven was like. She could just tell them to do good and feel good. She doesn't like children, but she might specialize in working with them. After decades of interacting with decrepit seniors, she might enjoy interacting with young people.

But changing careers would require her to go back to school. Does she really want to go through that again? She'd have to take out more loans. She'd have to complete the application process. She'd have to spend her evenings doing homework. She'd have to spend six or nine or twelve hours a week in class. She'd find herself sitting next to twentysomethings. The professor might even be younger than her.

The Old Testament book of *Ecclesiastes* tells us that "To every thing there is a season, and a time to every purpose under the heaven: a time to be born and a time to die; a time to plant, and a time to pluck up that which is planted." Likewise, there is a time to build a career and a time to resign oneself to the career one has built.

2. Kaye doesn't want to hear her mother say "I told you so".

HELEN MARTIN DISAPPROVED OF HER DAUGHTER'S ORDINATION. "Congregations deserve the composure and dignity of a man," she told her. "What are you going to do during your cycle, when you get crabby? What are you going to do the first time you have to bury an infant? The family will need someone strong, the way Jesus was strong. They won't need someone sobbing right next to them! The priest is the representative of Christ, and you're no Jesus! The moment you find that out, you'll feel embarrassed and walk away from it all. I don't want that for you."

Kaye's father (a retired dentist named Hank Martin) more or less went along with Kaye's mother. Truth be told, he really didn't care what Kaye did with her life. He wasn't a serious man. He went from one amusement to another: from the golf course to the club house, to his man cave, to

Hooters, and back again, always and everywhere with a glass of gin in his hand. He sided with Helen to keep the peace.

When Kaye insisted on attending seminary, Helen stopped going to church. Hank, never a big churchgoer to begin with, followed suit. When Kaye got ordained as an Episcopal priest, Helen converted to Catholicism. That was too much work for Hank. Instead, he used the extra free time for fantasy football. He took to wearing a Peyton Manning Colts jersey. He started wearing his baseball caps backwards.

Helen and Kaye talk once a month. Helen refuses to call Kaye a priest. (Helen now thinks only Catholics can legitimately call themselves priests.) If a friend asks Helen what her daughter does, she'll say: "She works for a church," and leave it at that. When Helen tries to make small talk with Kaye, she won't ask "How's your congregation?"; she'll ask "How's work?". Hank and Kaye barely talk at all. This isn't because of family tension, it's simply because he's always off amusing himself.

If Kaye were to tell her mother she'd left the priesthood, her mother would think she'd won. In reality she would not have won. Kaye wouldn't be leaving because she sobbed at the funeral of an infant, or because she had given vent to premenstrual fury at an inopportune time. However, her mother would *think* she had won, and Kaye wants to deprive her of even the *appearance* of victory.

3. Afterwards, she would feel the need to keep it secret.

KAYE SOMETIMES DAYDREAMS ABOUT THE SORT OF LIFE SHE'D lead if she left the priesthood. She imagines Charlie picking their new town at random, maybe by tossing a dart at a map. She imagines pulling up stakes and leaving before dawn. She imagines never telling anyone in their new town that she used to be a priest. Doing so would invite scrutiny. People would assume the worst: some scandal had gotten her defrocked.

Even if she made it clear she left the priesthood voluntarily, everyone would think something was wrong with her. The religious people would think something was wrong with her because clergy should always remain clergy. If a priest leaves the priesthood, then she must not have been *truly* called by God in the first place. If she had been, she would have stuck it out. On the other hand, the secular people would think something was wrong with her because she had joined the priesthood to begin with! To them, she would be a pathetic specimen, proof that religion is a waste of time. Get involved with it, and you'll eventually burn out. At least, you will if you have half a brain. The mental gymnastics one must perform to maintain faith in a two thousand year old book of folktales are too exhausting!

And what of the people in the middle, those who consider themselves "spiritual but not religious"? They, too, would look down on her. They would think she had only clung to organized religion out of cowardice. They would think she didn't trust her own, idiosyncratic, experiences with the transcendent. She had to find safety in the herd. Charlie sometimes lets on that he feels this way. He looks at her like a prisoner in an unlocked cell who refuses to open the door and leave.

4. The awful emptiness she would feel afterward.

EVERY HUMAN SOUL IS LIKE A DRINKING GLASS. IN CHILDHOOD, our parents pour notions into us. In adulthood, we spill such notions out. We seek out institutions, mentors, and causes that can pour new notions into us. The Episcopal Church poured the idea of priesthood into her. A beloved mentor,

Reverend Kate Williams, poured the specific, feminist idea of *women* priests into her. She would feel like a traitor if she poured these ideas out.

But the guilt wouldn't be the worst part. The emptiness would be the worst part. If she somehow managed to pour the priesthood out of herself, she would be empty. Charlie might then try to pour some of his paganism into her, but she doesn't want her own glass to be filled up by Charlie's. Something about that wouldn't feel right.

5. She would miss being in charge of the Holy Eucharist.

"THE EUCHARIST" IS THE EPISCOPAL SERVICE OF HOLY communion, the ritual in which the flock are made to believe they make contact with the "real presence" of Christ. Mother Kaye is designated the "celebrant" of the Eucharist. In its verb form, "celebrating the Eucharist" means, essentially, presiding over it.

Therefore, Mother Kaye is in charge of something sacred. Jesus might be the star, but she's the director. He can only appear if she says the magic words. This is a private thought of hers, not entirely consistent with Episcopal theology. In fact, it's probably heretical. But she has the thought and she likes having it so she doesn't shoo it away.

6. She would miss the altered state of consciousness she slips into when she celebrates the Eucharist.

I'VE JUST DESCRIBED THE *EXTERNAL* VALIDATION KAYE GETS FROM being a priest, the dopamine hit she gets from standing in the spotlight. Now let's talk about the dopamine hit she gets when she feels the actual presence of Christ *within her* during the communion service.

This can happen at any point during the Eucharist, but happens most frequently during the breaking of bread, when she utters the same words Christ uttered: "Take, eat: This is my Body, which is given for you. Do this for the remembrance of me." Then she takes a communion wafer and snaps it in half.

The church is quiet during this moment. No young families means no wailing infants. The acoustics make the crisp sound of wafer-breaking reverberate. It sounds like ice cracking in a glass of water, only much louder.

And when the wafer breaks, it sometimes feels like *time* is breaking. The millennia which separate Kaye from Jesus are obliterated. He, a first century Jew, is a ghost possessing her. Sometimes, though, it feels like she (a twenty-first century woman) is a ghost possessing Him. Sometimes, it feels like both are happening at the same time; like a case of mutual possession. (More heretical thoughts. She doesn't shoo these away, either. She enjoys them too much.)

Sometimes the mysticism has another wrinkle to it: she feels as though she is one half of God and Jesus of Nazareth is the other. The act of snapping apart that wafer breaks them in two. Then more magick happens. The two halves of the wafer go through rapid asexual reproduction. Before long there are enough wafters to go around the congregation. When she feeds the congregation the wafers, she's feeding them pieces of herself. Yes, pieces of herself and pieces of Jesus. Perhaps that's why she feels so empty on Sunday afternoons. She's been devoured. But the moment before the devouring, that moment when she feels time breaking, makes it all worthwhile.

7. Every once in a while a new theological fad emerges that makes Christianity seem doable.

In 2019, it was a movement called ChristDream. ChristDream's seminal text is a one hundred page book by Reverend Clinton Berry titled *God Dreams but Has No Nightmares*. It argued that Jesus was one of God's dreams and that Moses, Buddha, Krishna, and Mohammed were others.

"This may explain why the story of Christ seems both real and absurd," Father Berry wrote on page fifty-two. "Dreams are like that. We need to embrace the dreaminess of Christ. We joined the ChristDream by virtue of our baptism. At the same time, we must acknowledge the validity of other dreams. God is having more than one dream during this Long Night of Being. The mind of God is infinite. So, of course, His dreams are infinite, too.

"We have joined the ChristDream but our Muslim friends have joined the MohammedDream. Are we right? Are they wrong? No! But it makes sense that we have such a hard time getting along with each other. Citizens of one dream cannot understand the rules governing the citizens of another! Each dream has its own unique logic. We have a hard enough time explaining our prosaic nightly dreams to our spouses the next day. Why then, should we expect to understand the transcendent dreams of other cultures?

And then, on page seventy-five, he delivered the following gem.

"When you're in the midst of a dream, you don't second guess it. When you awaken, of course, it will seem odd to you. It will seem to be a thing separate *from* reality. But wouldn't it be more accurate to consider it *a separate reality*? The indigenous peoples of Australia call such separate realities 'dreamtime'. What can we, in the Episcopal Church, learn from aboriginal shamen? Can we make our faith more palatable to a secularized world by telling them the Good News that our services take place in this dreamtime? Can we stodgy Episcopalians accept God's gift of irrationality? Can we celebrate the dream? Can we acknowledge that Jesus wasn't *actually*, in waking reality, born of a virgin, but in *God's dream* he was?"

When Mother Kaye read that paragraph, her lifelong engagement with Christianity made sense! She was in bed with Charlie when she read it. She called his attention to it. He wasn't all that impressed. "The problem is it's still monotheism. There's only one true God and he's the one doing the dreaming. What about Pan? Can't he dream, too?"

Kaye pondered the question. "Why not?"

"Exactly. In fact, maybe *Pan* is dreaming of *Mr. One, True God*, and Mr. One, True God dreams of Christ. Maybe Persephone has dreamt up Pan! Preach that from the pulpit, and I'll come to church every week."

Kaye playfully bopped Charlie in the head with her book. At least, she'd *intended* to do it playfully. It actually left a red mark. In retaliation he gave her a hard pinch on her bottom. He then sunk his teeth into her neck and tried to grope her boobs. "*I* dream about fucking a priest," he said between slobbery nibbles. "How crazy is that?"

She slapped his hand away. The slap also left a red mark. As before, she hadn't *intended* to leave a mark. It just turned out that way. Once it was clear that Charlie wasn't as enthusiastic about ChristDream as she was, she turned her attention back to her book. The wisdom of Father Berry demanded her full attention.

She moved her brain into Berry's worldview and stayed there for several months. However, she never mentioned Berry's ideas in her sermons. After all, he was an innovator.

The gray heads in her pews resist innovation. If she dared to quote him from the pulpit, they would have thought she was abandoning her faith, instead of reaching a deeper layer of it. They may have even thought she was going mad! She didn't want to confuse the laity by preaching sophisticated ideas beyond their ken.

Also, she wanted to keep her job.

So, instead of mentioning Berry's ideas, she merely let herself move around the altar under their influence. Whenever something in the gospels seemed impossible, she told herself the New Testament was a dream. Lazarus was a character in this dream, and Jesus of Nazareth was another, and she, herself, was "a citizen" (so to speak) of the very same dream, two thousand years later.

Another metaphor: her brain was hardware. Theology was software (specifically, an operating system). Reading Berry's book installed his theological fad into her head. It automatically uninstalled the theological fad ("Quantum Crucifixion") that had preceded it. The new operating system made her a far more powerful preacher. She embraced the ChristDream. She allowed herself to become not only a citizen of that state but also a patriot for it. While up at the pulpit, dressed in her vestments and stole, she believed the myths were true. In the context of the dream, they *were* true. Well, true-*ish*. And she gave herself over to the dream each Sunday morning.

The congregation loved her newfound enthusiasm. She knew this because they told her so. They took her aside at coffee hour, smiled, and told her they noted a "new strength in (her) message". The well-to-do octogenarian widow told her the recent sermons reminded her of those given by the female televangelist Joyce Meyer. She meant it as a compliment. Mother Kaye, feeling a little queasy, accepted the praise with a fake smile. Week after week, she observed a slow increase in attendance. It had gotten as high as forty-two parishioners, in late February of 2020.

Then the pandemic ruined everything.

The governor ordered in-person church attendance to be limited to ten people. Several churches in town bucked the order. The cops weren't about to enforce it. Nonetheless, Mother Kaye's bishop expected St. Luke's to comply. And she did, because she respected the chain of command.

Also, she didn't want to lose her job.

So, she capped the in-person attendance at ten and tried to convince the rest to get onto Zoom. But it was all in vain. Everyone wanted to ignore the Governor and pretend nothing had changed. This led to many awkward conversations in the vestibule.

It was the worst experience of her career. It reminded her of the fast food jobs she worked as a teenager. A customer would ask for something impossible, and she would have to tell them it was impossible, and they would raise their voice and rain sarcasm down on her. Here she was, a middle aged professional, dealing with the same thing.

"You're turning me away at the door?" some shriveled half-corpse of a man would say.

"The Governor has limited in-person attendance to ten people."

"You're turning me away *at the door*?!" the mummy would repeat.

The second Sunday, not a single congregant showed up for in-person services and only six showed up on Zoom. Had she persuaded twelve to join her, it might have felt auspicious. They would have been her twelve disciples. Six, however, is a bad omen. (She'd learned that from Charlie.)

The Zoom service didn't go well. It got bombed. As Mother Kaye bellowed "The Lord be with you," a young man responded "Nobody cares, woman." He then proceeded to share a pornographic video from his screen.

Mother Kaye wasn't responsible for any of this, of course. And yet, she received all the blame. None of it would have happened if St. Luke's had continued to hold services in person, like all the other churches in town.

The governor ended most of the restrictions on face-to-face church attendance in early May. The Bishop of Southern Indiana, however, felt this was unsafe. He required St. Luke's to convene a "Regathering Committee" charged with the drafting of a "Regathering Plan" listing all the anti-COVID safeguards they would be taking. Once the plan was approved by the Diocese, the doors could reopen.

Mother Kaye explained all of this in an email to the vestry (the church's advisory board of laypeople).

It didn't go over well.

"They had all sorts of diseases in Jesus' time," Dave Garland (the church treasurer) replied, "and He didn't make the disciples wear masks!" Other vestry members couched their objections in less dramatic terms: they simply chafed under the yoke of bureaucracy.

The Regathering Committee ended up with only three members: Mother Kaye, her laptop, and the cat. It reminded her of the many times in high school when she did all the work on a group project.

Only this was far worse. In high school, the slackers didn't try to micromanage her. At St. Luke's, however, the vestry demanded veto power over the plan. The vestry held veto power, and the Bishop held veto power. Mother Kaye held no power. She was a pawn in an anarchic chess game: both players claimed her as their piece.

She still subscribed to ChristDream, as a theory. She re-read Father Berry's book and it made her brain tingle. But it no longer made her heart soar.

She began giving in to certain un-Christlike habits. When she was talking to the Bishop's staffers she maligned her vestry. When she was talking to the vestry she maligned the Bishop's staffers. She knew it was a sin to behave in such a two-faced manner. She knew it, and scolded herself, but kept right on doing it.

In early June, the two sides finally arrived at a compromise: outdoor services would be permitted. The church had a small courtyard that could be used for such purposes. Twenty people showed up for the first week, but the next week it rained and the following week it rained, and even though they'd erected a small tent for the purpose only three people showed up. And that's when ChristDream stopped making her brain tingle. That's when her brain started to feel heavier and slower, more tangled up in itself.

But she doesn't quit, because she knows another book will come along to offer a new handhold for her faith. Granted, it might still be two or three years away. But eventually her spiritual dry spell will end. Some new theological fad will emerge from the wilderness and place Christiniaty in a fresh context that will make it seem true (or, at least, *true enough*). This has always been the case, and it will continue to be the case. In the meantime she goes through the motions and waits. She waits in much the same way her Fundamentalist brethren await the second coming of Christ.

The Town of Owlingsville

p until now the name of Mother Kaye's town has remained unspoken. One could not be blamed for assuming the name is unimportant, that it is the *quintessential* Midwestern small town, a place of median angst and arithmetically mean fortunes.

This is not so.

Each of Indiana's small towns has its own personality, in the same way each child in a family has its own personality. True, some personality traits occur, to varying degrees, in each. But, overall, the differences outweigh the similarities.

St. Luke's Episcopal Church is in Owlingsville. You may be tempted to pronounce it "Owl-ings-ville" but the locals say "Owe-lings-ville". Throughout the years many unfunny jokes have been cracked about it sounding like "Owing Bills". (The joke being that everyone in town is up to their asscracks in debt.) But it doesn't really sound like "Owing Bills", does it? Maybe a drunk slurring their speech would make it sound like "Owing Bills", but no one else would. That's the kind of town this is: even its efforts at self-deprecation fall flat.

Owlingsville isn't close to the Ohio River, the Great Lakes, or any major city. (Charlie has to drive well over an hour to get to the closest of his pagan meetups.)

You can *breathe* in a city. The air might smell of sewage, but you still breathe easy because nobody knows who you are. It might be more crowded, but you're less noticeable. It lowers your blood pressure, to move around with so much privacy.

You can also breathe in a small town, provided it has a sufficiently expansive waterfront. Yes, the streets and homes and apartments and trailer parks are claustrophobic and suffocating, but you can get a natural pick-me-up by wandering off to some lonesome river bank. The breeze coming off the water lowers your blood pressure, too.

Rivers flow through Owlingsville, of course. It's not a desert. But they're sad, narrow, polluted rivers. Tributaries, really, not rivers in their own right. They exert no positive influence on the soul. Likewise, privacy is impossible. Everyone in town is cheering for the humiliation, if not the outright ruin, of their neighbors. Well, maybe not *everyone*. But most people. Owlinsgville is a place where people keep score. Arrests, overdoses, messy divorces and wayward children are tallied up on a regular basis. As long as your family has fewer than your neighbors', you win.

For several decades, the chief employer in Owlingsville was a gypsum mining concern called Owling Resources. (Gypsum is a fire-resistant mineral used in the manufacture of drywall.) If there were any mercy at work in the universe, Owlingsville would have died in the nineties. That's when its mine was all played out. The old goose had no more golden eggs inside her.

The state stepped in, though. It wouldn't let the town die with dignity. It built a new prison (strictly for violent men) on the outskirts of town and contracted out the running of its operations to a corporation called CSG (The Civic Salus Group, a name derived from the Latin words for "city" and "safety"). It also built a psychiatric hospital. That one is run by the state, though, and goes by the unimaginative moniker "Owlingsville State Hospital".

Townsfolk prefer to work at the hospital because state employees get better benefits, but aside from that difference it really isn't a better workplace. Both the prison and the hospital keep people locked up against their will. Both teem with violence and foulness. An institution is an institution, regardless of its mission statement. They have more similarities than differences.

Working in an institution does something to a person. It pours ugliness into their soul. When a *whole town* depends on this ugliness, life turns harsh and crass. It would be tempting to add the adjective "humorless" to this list, but the prison guards and hospital orderlies get a kick out of ridiculing their charges. So, the townsfolk do have occasion to laugh.

Owlingsville has an entrepreneurial class, as well. A handful of men have started their own auto repair businesses. There are independent housing contractors and construction companies, one fast food franchise (Subway), a handful of Mom & Pop restaurants, and thrift stores too.

And, of course, there's a Wal-Mart.

Among the congregation at St. Luke's you will currently find three members of the Owling family. There used to be many more, of course. The Owlings and St. Luke's have always enjoyed a special relationship. In fact, Father Abbott's predecessor, Father Claggett, used to don a hardhat, descend into the underworld, and perform a brief "Blessing of the

Mines" service each September. Every year, he beseeched the good Lord to grant the Owlings and their workers "safe and profitable operations".

Even though Owling Resources is a thing of the past, and the Owlings could afford to live in more pleasant surroundings, they remain in town. Perhaps they enjoy being big fish in a small bowl.

The octogenarian widow who mistakenly calls Mother Kaye "Mary Kay" comes from this clan. Her name is Anne Owling. She barely survived a heart attack last Christmas Eve, and is not expected to live long. Nonetheless, she has enough pep to complain when the service isn't to her liking. Nobody knows what's in her will, but Mother Kaye remains hopeful that a large bequest will fall into the church's hands. That would buy the congregation at least another twenty years of financial security.

Others in attendance include retired teachers, social workers, and psychologists. (The Episcopal Church doesn't just serve the spiritual needs of old money, it attracts impractical do-gooders too.) Much outnumbered in a town full of prison guards, they cling together for mutual support. They cluster together at coffee hour to discuss matters only they will understand.

Then there are certain oddballs, congregants who seem utterly miscast as Episcopalians. For example, the aforementioned church treasurer, Dave Garland, is as dedicated a parishioner as can be found. Volunteers all the time. Why? It makes no sense! He's the head accountant for CSG-Owlingsville. He's a mover and shaker in the local Republican party. His networking opportunities would be far greater if he attended All-American Resurrection Church. (Yes, that's the actual name of the place.)

"All-American" (the preferred truncation of the name) is Owlingsville's biggest hive of fundamentalism. It's not yet a megachurch. Only about four hundred folks show up each week. But it clearly aspires to that status. It follows the same game plan as all the others. Pastor Wayne Wright has turned his services into full-fledged Trump rallies. He also posts weekly rants on YouTube. So far, he's only averaging forty views.

In fairness, this may have more to do with the technical quality of his videos rather than their content. The audio is horrible. His camera wobbles. He was a grocery store manager before he heard God's call, so video production doesn't come to him naturally. He's a savvy businessman, though. When he founded the church he knew he should give it a name that started with the letter A. That way, it would always be listed first in the phone book.

Well, actually, there's one other church in town that starts with the letter A: All Saints Lutheran. That's why he specifically went with *"All-American* Resurrection Church". "All-American" is alphabetically ahead of "All Saints".

And speaking of other churches, now is as good a time as any to mention Owlingsville's ethnic minorities. The Census says 0.5% of the town is African-American. Nearly all attend Mt. Moriah A.M.E. Church. The A.M.E. stands for African Methodist Episcopal. Dave Garland once went to great pains to explain to Mayor Duncan that *his* Episcopal Church had "absolutely zero (sic) to do with the Blacks".

Actually, there is one Black member of St. Luke's: a shy young man named Erik. He was adopted by one of the social workers. He's seventeen and, like most seventeen year olds, only shows up on Christmas and Easter (and even then under great duress). He dreams of drawing comics for Marvel. He's quite good, actually.

Immigrants from Mexico and Central America have found Owlingsville. The low cost of living attracts them. However, they've never quite managed to flourish there. The cops go out of their way to hassle them, so they never stay long. Police Chief Darryl Minter encourages his officers to target them for traffic stops. "They've already broken the law once by coming here in the first place," Minter tells them. "So of course they need to be watched."

Skin color does not constitute probable cause for a search. If Owlingsville were a city, or even within a fifty mile radius of one, such sentiments would perhaps leak out and stir opposition. But Owlingsville is Owlingsville. Anti-immigrant prejudice is the townsfolk's default setting. Only a few have managed to change it, and they are too timid to speak out. Doing so would separate them from the herd.

Outsiders *of any sort* are eyed with suspicion. An "immigrant" from Indianapolis would be disdained simply because no one would know where to place them in the hierarchy. It bears repeating: Owlinsgville is a place where people keep score. Arrests, overdoses, messy divorces and wayward children are tallied up on a regular basis. As long as your family has fewer than your neighbors', you win.

So what do you do with someone new to town? Someone who doesn't disclose their family's history of arrests, overdoses, messy divorces, and wayward children? Someone who has no experience (or worse yet, no *interest*) in playing such games. It would be like welcoming a cricket team into the NFL. They would be on the same field, but they wouldn't understand the rules. They would be playing their game while you were playing yours. You could run the ball eighty yards for a touchdown but the moment would be meaningless because they wouldn't know they were supposed to stop you.

An Email Arrives from the Diocesan Administrator for Congregational Vitality

To: Reverend Heather Kaye Ford (MotherKaye@ stlukesowlingsville.org)

From: Reverend Erika Grossman, Congregational Vitality Facilitator, Diocese of Southern Indiana (EGrossman@ EpiscopalDioceseSIndiana.org)

Date: June 14, 2020

Re: Fwd: Outdoor Services Unexpected Blessing for Bay Area Churches

Dear Kaye:
This sounds like a smart path for St. Luke's to follow during these uncertain times. I know you've tried services in your courtyard, but moving them to a public park might yield greater benefits. Even if congregational participation is limited, it allows you to preach the gospel to anyone visiting the park.

My hope is that you will prayerfully consider taking this step. I encourage you to forward this onto your vestry for their consideration.

Yours in Christ,
Rev. Erika

THE FORWARDED ARTICLE DESCRIBES HOW A NONBINARY PRIEST in San Francisco named Rev. Binx Stratford decided to celebrate the Holy Eucharist each Sunday afternoon for homeless queer youth in Golden Gate Park.

"'At first we were treated like oddities,' Reverend Stratford said. 'People jeered at us, which is understandable. We were treading on their turf. But once they understood we weren't there to condemn them, we were grudgingly tolerated. That was the first revolution. And the second came soon afterwards: they noticed our entire congregation is queer. In fact one of the women on our vestry is a sex worker. So we not only *didn't condemn them*, we *were them*. Once they recognized that fact, the Holy Spirit found a home in their hearts.'"

THERE'S NO WAY MOTHER KAYE CAN FORWARD SUCH A testimonial to her vestry. Does Reverend Erika not understand this? No one at St. Luke's would even be able to *understand* the article. Few, if any, have been exposed to the notion of the gender continuum. (If they have, it would be through Tucker Carlson, who would have discussed it as an example of "gender insanity".)

Furthermore, the reference to "sex workers" would baffle and embarrass them. They would think it had been a typo. Surely, the article was meant to read "sea workers", as in fishermen or merchant marines? The "a" key is not that far from the "x" key. That would be their explanation.

Then it would fall on Mother Kaye to correct them. "Actually," she imagines herself explaining, "that's no typo. They mean sex workers."

And then Anne Owling would start chirping. "Surely you don't mean pros…"

And Mother Kaye would have to interrupt the bipedal checkbook mid-sentence (something otherwise unthinkable) so the unfortunate word wouldn't be said. "Yes, that's what Reverend Stratford means," she'd say. And then she would try to take the edge off the article. She would try to place it in the context of the gospel story of Jesus allowing a…sex worker… to wash His feet with her tears and dry them with her hair.

But, of course, Anne Owling wouldn't buy it. And, who knows, it might even disgust her to the point where she would take her checkbook elsewhere. Mother Kaye knows this is unlikely, though. If middle aged inertia is a thing, then octogenarian inertia is, too. Anne Owling has inordinate sway over the goings on at St. Luke's, and it would be difficult to capture that much power as an elderly newcomer to a church like All-American. Moreover, she's temperamentally ill-at-ease with holy rollers. The screaming from the pulpit would get on her nerves. It's gauche. Perhaps this is the reason Dave Garland remains an Episcopalian, too. For a certain kind of conservative, the Episcopal Church has snob appeal. The Church hierarchy might be dominated by liberals, but at least they're limousine liberals. And the Anne Owlings and Dave Garlands of the world prefer the company of limousine liberals to that of pickup truck fundamentalists.

Mother Kaye Tries to Do Something

An idea occurs to Mother Kaye: she doesn't have to pass along the news article in order to suggest holding services in a public park. She could frame it as an idea of her own.

That way, she wouldn't have to say the idea came from the diocese. Nor would she have to acquaint her vestry with Binx Stratford, queer youth, and sex workers.

She sends an email.

The replies from the vestry trickle in over the course of a week. They all seem slightly taken aback. They aren't used to Mother Kaye taking the initiative. Mother Kaye knows this, and feels embarrassed about having made the attempt. Nobody wants to hold services in a public park. The vestry thinks it's impractical. Lots of "It's a good idea, but…". Take these three responses, for example.

"It's a good idea, but they have moles in that field. The ground is unsteady and our people could easily fall there. Would our liability coverage extend to such a service? We wouldn't want to get sued because someone broke a hip out there."

"I have often wondered if this might not be a way to move forward, but the only facilities out there are port-a-potties. Hardly appropriate, I think you'll agree."

"If you had brought this to us a month ago, we might have been able to do something. My understanding is that All-American has it reserved for the next several months. Not because they want to be safe from COVID, but because they're starting to run out of room in that building. They're doing services in their church building *and* in the park, connected through Zoom. They haven't had any incidents with it, the way we did."

Ordinarily, Kaye would have retreated into herself after such a defeat. Each dismissive email would have been a nail in her cross, torturing and immobilizing her. She would have gone home, ate a half-gallon of ice cream, and tried to forget the whole thing. This time, however, something within her won't relent.

Something within her? Really? Perhaps it's something *outside* of her! Or some*one* outside of her. The Holy Spirit, for example. Yes, that might be a better way of looking at it.

Or maybe she's just trying to keep Reverend Erika happy.

Whatever the case may be, when the vestry refuses to greenlight her pitch, she immediately sends them another. "You all make very solid points," she replies. "It's best to start small. Instead of having Sunday services at the park, I'll simply show up at the park each day at sunset, find a bench, and pray with anyone who wants to join me. I'll call it 'Prayer in the Park' (or maybe 'Pray with Kaye')."

Over the course of the next three hours she refreshes her email five times. No replies. She checks again before bedtime. Still no replies. When she wakes up she checks again. Nothing. She takes the vestry's stunned silence as consent. When she goes into the office, she adds an announcement to the church bulletin. She even uses money from her discretionary fund to buy an advertisement in the June 17, 2020 edition of the *Owlingsville Courier*.

PRAYER IN THE PARK
JUNE 20th - JULY 31

JOIN MOTHER KAYE (ST. LUKE'S EPISCOPAL CHURCH)

FOR A TIME OF PRAYER AND REFLECTION IN PATRIOT PARK

MONDAY-SATURDAY, STARTING THIRTY MINUTES BEFORE SUNSET

JUST LOOK FOR THE LADY PRIEST ON A BENCH!

She doesn't even bother asking the park for permission. Nor does she run it past Charlie. (Evenings are their time to connect, to enjoy each other's company, to read or take a walk or play with their cat or make love. Saturday evenings are supposed to be *especially* off-limits. That's their date night.) But it's only for six weeks, and if she prays loud enough, she might be able to include any random passerby in her attendance figures. *That* would keep the diocese happy.

The Storm

It's the longest day of the year. The sun isn't supposed to set until 9:10. However, there is no sun. Or rather, there is a sun, but it's dying. The rain's drowning it. The lightning's stabbing it. The clouds are poisoning it.

So, you can imagine Charlie's exasperation when Kaye grabs her car keys at 8:30. "You're not going *out* in this mess," he says.

"I made a commitment. It's in the paper."

"No one reads the *Courier* anymore."

"I think they put it on the website, too."

"Yeah, but you'll get drenched."

"There's a pavilion. I'll hang out there until the rain stops."

Charlie stabs his finger at his phone. Examines the screen. "It's supposed to last for another two hours. You can try again tomorrow if you want."

You can try again tomorrow. Like he's granting her *permission* to try again tomorrow. Like he's talking to a child who wants to play outside.

Kaye feels her blood pressure rise. "Were you even listening to me? I told you I'll hang out at the pavilion until the rain stops."

"Yeah, but no one will look for you there. And no one will blame you for not showing up."

And Kaye knows he's probably right, but she doesn't care. She's now obsessed with getting out to Patriot Park. It's a matter of pride. She can't let herself be pushed around by Charlie. It's also a matter of fear. What if someone sees the ad in the paper and, propelled by desperation, makes the trip out in the rain to pray? What if they get there and find no "lady priest" to pray with?

All-American Resurrection Church wouldn't let a little rain prevent them from holding an event. What they lack in brains they make up for in determination. Do they appreciate nuance? No. But nuance is the mother of uncertainty, dithering, and weakness. Yeats foresaw this situation: "The best lack all conviction, while the worst / Are full of passionate intensity."

Mother Kaye refuses to prove Yeats right. She dons a yellow raincoat and yellow plastic hat. It's the sort of outfit a six year old would wear. A six year old, or a fisherman. On top of her gray slacks and black clergy shirt, the coat looks especially ridiculous. Kaye doesn't care. A strange thought creeps through her mind: *This is the perfect outfit, because I'm leaving my safe harbor to be a fisher of men, just like Jesus and his disciples.* Fueled by this off-kilter confidence, she grabs an umbrella from the closet and says goodbye to Charlie. "I'll be back around nine-thirty. Love you."

Charlie sighs. Stabs his finger at his phone again. He seems to be looking for some video or meme to take his mind off the argument. "Love you, too," he says.

Mother Kaye Hears a Confession

The drive to the park is nerve racking (because of the downpour). It's also relaxing (because she's away from Charlie). It takes only ten minutes to get there. She hydroplanes out into the intersection of Church and Maple streets, but no one else is on the road. She arrives at the park and marches toward the pavilion. It's farther from the parking lot than she remembers.

The ground has turned marshy. Her shoes aren't up to the task. Her socks get drenched. Her feet get cold. Each raindrop is a liquid dart, and a hundred slap her every second. When they hit the hard plastic of her coat they sound like hail. They're not hail, though; just hard drops of rain. When they hit her skin they sting. On top of it all, her arthritis always flares up when it's damp. Her knuckles have swollen.

The pavilion boasts ten picnic tables. It's the kind of place parents reserve for their kids' summer birthday parties. She finds a trash bag resting atop one of the tables. It wobbles to life. "Pardon me miss, but can you spare some change? There's a hole in my pocket and I lost my bus fare." The trash bag's voice is high pitched, squeaky, and male.

No, the trash bag isn't talking. The voice belongs to a derelict *wearing a trash bag* as a makeshift raincoat. He's lifting his head off the table now and Kaye can see his face. Before, his face had been obscured. So, it's understandable that Kaye would have thought, for a split second, that the trash bag was talking to her. You would have been confused, as well, if you had seen and heard what Kaye had.

Now the man rises from his seat and approaches, revealing ragged pants and hole-ridden sneakers. He reeks of rum. Kaye knows his story is spurious. Owlingsville has no bus system. He's probably a recent alumnus of the state hospital. Probably comes from a city that doesn't want him back. He resorts to using his old panhandling line. He doesn't realize how easily it's debunked in his new town. Or perhaps he knows it isn't convincing, but doesn't care.

Kaye digs into her pockets, but has no change. She decides to grab her purse, maybe even give him some cash. But the purse isn't there. She was so distracted by her argument with Charlie that she forgot to grab it. So, for the moment, she feels every bit as penniless as the panhandler.

"I'm afraid I don't have any money right now. I mean, you probably hear that a lot but in my case it's absolutely true."

The panhandler rears back his head and laughs, exposing teeth that...look perfect. They're inexplicably white and straight. His teeth look better than Charlie's. They look better than her own. In fact, they are not actually teeth. They're *capped* teeth or dental veneers.

"In fact I do hear that a lot, mostly from studios who use creative accounting to deprive me of my fair share. 'There are no profits,' they always say. 'That high box office gross doesn't reflect our expenses. It takes a lot of cash to market a picture.'"

Kaye lets out a little groan.

Why does she groan? Because she has been taken by surprise, and she doesn't like it. The one benefit of living in a town like Owlingsville is that it offers few surprises. The one benefit of being middle aged is that you've seen it all. The one benefit of being an Episcopalian is that every Sunday is more or less the same; the same words read over and over from the same book. Perhaps, if she'd lived in a city, or if she were younger, or if she were a Baptist, she wouldn't be so rattled by the unexpected.

"I'm an actor," the pseudo-panhandler says, "doing research for my next role. I'll be playing an opioid addict. Quentin's directing."

Kaye lets out another groan. This one's deeper, darker.

Why does she groan a second time? Why is it a more awful groan? Because the absurdity of the situation concusses her soul. *And* because the rain is coming down even harder now. Sheets of water now encase her in the pavilion. She can see nothing outside of it. A watery membrane surrounds it. She feels *trapped* in the absurdity.

Her knees are starting to ache, as well as her knuckles. She sits down at one of the tables. Her legs can no longer support her.

The man takes a seat across from her. Points at her collar. "So, you're a pastor?" he asks.

"A p-priest," Kaye says.

"Women can't be priests," the pseudo-panhandler says. "So you're an actor, too, in a sense."

Once again, the annoying confusion over Episcopal priests. "In my denomination, women have been able to be priests for many years."

The pseudo-panhandler takes out a cigarette and cracked Bic lighter. Makes smoke and fire. "Would you like one, Madre?"

Kaye shakes her head.

"Me neither, but my character smokes. So, the way I see it, I need to play around with the habit. Wouldn't it be a hoot if I actually got hooked?" He giggles.

Kaye tries to giggle too. It ends up becoming a cough. The situation embarrasses her. She's not certain she believes this man is an actor. By the way he talks, he's quite a famous one. Surely, film producers don't offer a share of the profits to bit players. And yet, she doesn't recognize him. Moreover, if he were an actor preparing for a role, wouldn't he have kept the illusion going a little longer? It's strange for him to drop the facade so quickly.

Maybe he's a former patient of the state hospital, in thrall to delusions of grandeur. But then there's the matter of those perfect pseudo-teeth, those caps or veneers or whatever. A homeless man, afflicted with a severe mental illness, couldn't afford them.

Or could he? Perhaps he got them when he was young, before his illness hit its stride. Perhaps he *was* a promising young actor whose career was tragically cut short by psychosis. Or perhaps he came from a wealthy family who were embarrassed by his poor dental hygiene. Yes, that's it: he had neglected himself and they were embarrassed so they paid for the veneers. And how did he repay them? He wandered off.

To paraphrase Walt Whitman, this man contains multitudes. He's a kaleidoscope of being; his soul is always

46

shifting, flipping, into something new. Kaye's brain can't fathom him.

She, on the other hand, is rather dull in comparison. She's a priest. That's who she is. She might not be a very good priest, but she's a priest. She does not contain multitudes. She is, rather, *contained within* a tired, dying institution: the Episcopal Church.

And there's no way she can flee from this man who is more than one man. The rain pours worse than ever, building four hard walls of water all around the pavilion. She's locked in with him. The world outside is cold and wet, gray and wounding.

Besides, she made a commitment to stay here until sundown. She can't go until grayness has yielded to blackness. She came here for a reason. Yes, now she remembers the reason she's here. She'd gotten so wrapped up in the conversation that she nearly forgot.

"I came to the park to pray," she says. "Would you like to pray with me?"

The man wearing the trash bag exhales a cloud of smoke. Taps some ashes down onto the pavilion's cement floor. Smirks. "You're not gonna pray for rain, are you?"

The comment takes Kaye by surprise. She feels hurt. The man's question sounds condescending. He thinks *she* thinks rain comes from God (not from cold fronts). He thinks her brain is stuck in the bronze age. She tries to pretend she doesn't feel upset; tries to sound confident.

"That's not what I had in mind," she says.

"Well, what do you have in mind?"

A good question, to which Kaye has no answer. She has been preoccupied with the *administrivia* of bringing prayer to the park (fielding Reverend Erika's email, adapting her suggestion into something more palatable to her vestry, and placing the advertisement in the *Courier*). She has been focused on slick roads and drenched socks. She hasn't given any thought to the *content* of the prayers she would say. Upon realizing this, she feels foolish. A wave of self-criticism crests over her, threatening to crash. She tries to answer his question, but she can't.

Ordinarily, such an oversight would pose no problem for an Episcopalian. Their *Book of Common Prayer* not only offers a script for each week's service, it provides a plethora of prayers for various occasions. An Episcopalian never has to improvise. Unfortunately, Kaye not only forgot her purse, she forgot her prayer book too. That wave of self-criticism engulfs her now, batters her like the blows of a hundred hammers.

"Hey," the man says, "I have an idea. Priests hear confessions, right?"

"Well, the Episcopal Church doesn't emphasize confession in the same way the Catholics do, but we have a service called *Reconciliation of a Penitent*…"

"That's not what I'm driving at, Madre. I've never, ever, done anything wrong."

Mother Kaye smirks. "We've all done things we shouldn't have done, and we've all failed to do things we should have done. Anyway, I don't understand what you're trying to say. If you've never done anything wrong, what do you need to confess?"

"Well, I mean, I suppose I did lie to you by pretending to be homeless. Nothing could be further from the truth. The whole world is my home! But I had a good reason for lying. If I had just shown up in my true form, you would have gone mad. And I also lied to you when I let on that I was a Hollywood actor. But you have to understand, it's kind of my schtick to always show two faces to those who meet me. Either literally, like one of those so-called Siamese twins, or figuratively, as in: two different appearances in sequence. And besides, the Hollywood star persona was true, sort of, metaphorically. An actor is always changing roles, progressing from one identity to the next. So, that's as good a way as any to introduce myself. See, I'm no big time actor, but I am a star. Well, not a star, really, but one of the moons of Jupiter."

"I'm....sorry?" Kaye is hoping she heard him wrong.

"I mean, I'm not actually that moon, but they named that moon after me. Which kinda sucks, when you think about it. I mean, why should they name a planet after Jupiter, but only give me one of his moons? *I'm* the one who still's living! But I suppose that's just another aspect of my complexity: invisible in the night sky, visible everywhere on Earth."

Word salad. Schizophrenia. She's seen it before in Owlingsville. Mentally healthy people don't sit in a park, in the rain, claiming to be celestial objects. Then again, some might say that only a madwoman would sit in a park, in the rain, offering to hear the confession of a madman.

He takes another drag off his cigarette. Exhales. The smoke obscures everything but his veneers. She feels a tap on her hand. Sees those teeth raise and lower as he speaks. "I confess to you that this is not my true form."

Kaye leans back. Crosses her arms over her chest, so he can't touch her hand again; lets out an incredulous "Beg pardon?"

A breeze comes along and blows the smoke away.

"I am Janus. At least, that's what they used to call me in the days of Caesar. I keep the world churning. I keep *people* churning. I'm in charge of beginnings and endings, transitions, and doorways. I can make people go mad, and I can make them well again. So you best listen to what I have to say!

"I'm the one who makes *countries* go mad, too! I suppose you could say I put the geist in zeitgeist! I'm the only god left. All the others are dead. This world is a graveyard of gods! By the way, this might seem like it's coming from left field, but do you happen to have any change?"

Kaye can't help sighing in exasperation. (A very un-Christlike sigh.) "I told you already, no!"

He grabs her shoulders. Shakes her and stares in her eyes. Preaches a gospel of his own. "And that's exactly my point! You don't have Change, but you need Change. You're overdue for a change. And I'm here to inform you that it's long past time for you to leave the priesthood. As soon as I saw that advertisement in the *Courier*, I knew I had to come out here and face you.

"I'm the one who's been whispering into your soul for years, trying to persuade you that it's just not working. The church is a round hole and you're a square peg. Perhaps, back in your twenties you were round, too. But you're not anymore. You haven't been round in a long time. And you can pretend to be something you're not for only so long. It's not sustainable."

He stands up, walks a few feet away, and attempts a clownish cartwheel. He lands on his head. "Heed my warning: mental gymnastics is a sport that ends in mental injuries. I'm offering you the gift of reality. Accept your limitations! Accept the reality that you're not really a Christian, in the generally accepted sense. Accept the reality that each week, when you recite the Nicene Creed as part of the Eucharist, you're lying. You believe in, well, Something. But not Jesus. Accept this reality, resign your post first thing tomorrow morning, and delight in what freedom has to offer.

But bear in mind that I am not to be disrespected. Should you reject this gift I offer you tonight, I'll have no choice but to withdraw it. Reject reality and I will burden you with its absence."

He coughs. Catches his breath. Sits down at the table. Stretches. Giggles to himself. "I know that's a lot to take in all at once, but you know Hollywood these days. No time for the slow burn. I think Quentin's gonna want me to shout the lines real fast, like a rapper. Like, maybe I'm a homeless guy who thinks he's Vanilla Ice. I hear he might cast the real Vanilla Ice as a cop who kicks me out of the park. Quentin likes to pull that stunt casting shit, you know.

"Anyway, thanks for letting me unburden myself. I feel better already. Now that the rain's let up, I suppose I'll be making tracks. Take it easy, now."

As he's leaving, she feels someone tapping her on the shoulder. It's a skinny, bespectacled, half-bald old man in clerical garb. "Admit it, my child," Father Abbott's ghost says. "He has a point."

Stiffness

It's dark now. It's stopped raining. Kaye is still sitting at the picnic table. Charlie is pleading for her to leave.

"What's wrong, honey? Kaye? Let's go home."

She doesn't acknowledge his presence.

"The park's closed honey. It's after eleven. They arrest folks for trespassing here after dark."

"Go away." She feels the words spurt out of her mouth. Hears them being said. But it doesn't feel like she's the one saying them.

"Honey, please."

"Go away!"

Charlie flinches and crosses his arms. He sighs, impatiently. "Damnit, honey, let it go! I'm not the bad guy here. I tried to tell you no one would show up."

She shakes her head. A hollow whisper escapes her lips. "Someone was here. I heard his confession." Then she rises and makes her way to the parking lot.

Her gait is stiff, more of a shuffle than a walk. She loses her footing. She has stepped on a worm and slipped on its guts. The ground must be saturated. It came up for air. She didn't mean to kill it. She scrapes her shoe against the cement to get it off.

"Hey, here are your keys," Charlie says. "I found them under the table. You're okay to drive, right?"

She isn't, not really. Her arthritis is too severe, her movements too constrained, her brain too fuzzy. But she wants to be done with this place, so she takes the keys in her hand. Starts up her car. Follows the man named Charlie to the place called home.

Sick Day

Her world is a bed. She only sees the sun when it's filtered through off-white sheets. This seems cozy, or at least tolerable. The air conditioning isn't working as well as it should, but she doesn't care. The stuffy air seems appropriate. She has been put away in storage. She is an obsolete computer. She will not be able to work unless something deep inside her is fixed.

Charlie knocks on the door a few times. Brings her cereal and coffee. She takes a few nibbles, a few sips, and lets the rest go to waste. He asks her questions. She gives perfunctory answers.

"What's wrong?"

"I'm tired."

"Do you think you might have COVID?"

"I think I'm tired."

"Why are you so pissy?"

"Why are you so pushy?"

"Do you think maybe you should see a doctor?"

"I think I need to be alone."

"What am I supposed to tell the vestry? The meeting's tonight."

"It's Tuesday?"

"Uh huh. Lunchtime. Maggie came over to see where you were. You were supposed to attend a Zoom call with the Diocese at ten. I told her you went out to the park last night and that you seem to have caught a cold."

She looks at her phone. *12:23.*

The homeless actor, Janus, said she should resign first thing in the morning. She's slept past the deadline. Should she be worried?

Her first thought: *No, I shouldn't be worried. If Janus was just a hallucination, then his ultimatums have no teeth. If Janus wasn't a hallucination, then his ultimatum is irrelevant because he's not the god I serve.*

Her second thought: *Yes, I should be worried. If Janus was just a hallucination, then I'm going nuts. If Janus wasn't a hallucination, then perhaps the god I serve is dead. He* did *say all the other gods were dead, right? Did he just mean all the other gods in his* pantheon? *All the other Roman gods? Or did he mean he was the only god of any sort who still lives? That would explain a lot. The only constant is Change.*

"Honey, are you okay?"

"I'm just tired."

"This isn't like you."

"I'm not like me," she agrees. Then she turns onto her side and falls asleep again.

She naps in ninety minute spurts, wakes up for an hour, then crashes again. Some people would find this annoying, but Kaye doesn't. She actually prefers it because there's no longer any rigid line separating wakefulness from sleep. Sleep blends into wakefulness and vice-versa. Neither state of consciousness is able to declare victory. Somehow, that seems right.

So, it can't rightly be said that she dreams. She half-dreams. And, after she half-dreams, she half *day*dreams. Sometimes she imagines she's Father Claggett down in the damp gypsum mine, making the sign of the cross over a sea of hardhats and heavy drilling equipment. Other times she imagines she's Willy Abbott playing golf up in Indianapolis with Jack Owling. She's complimenting Jack on his taste in clubs. "A top-drawer selection. I simply must get a set just like them!"

She wakes up disappointed. She's not Father Claggett. She's not Willy Abbott. She never will be.

The self-loathing is a heavy burden. She can't bear it much longer. Another wave of slumber half-engulfs her. A half-dream follows. She's going off with Charlie to a small family owned hotel. They have to drive thirty miles through winding, hilly country roads to get there. There's a diner in the front of the building. Behind the kitchen there's a large room. Their room. It has four doors (one on each wall).

Sometimes, people come in unannounced. Charlie yells at them. Kaye tells Charlie to cool it. (Those are the words she uses: "Cool it!") She explains to him that no one is trying to disrupt their getaway. The hotel explained, after all, that this room usually isn't rented out. The kitchen and housekeeping staff use it as their break room. The hotel only rents it out when there's no other room available, and the owners only charge them half of what they'd pay for a normal room.

Charlie starts wailing and pulling his hair. Kaye half-wakes. Half-wishes she were half-dead. Imagines she *is* half-dead. Imagines herself wrapped in an antique lace shroud. No, it's not lace. Nor is it a shroud. It's spiderwebs. Spiders skitter through her esophagus. Their footfalls are light, but sticky.

The lace is really a spider web. No, the spider web is actually a threadbare sheet. Actually, the threadbare sheet is the skin of a ghost. Yes, a ghost is nothing more than an animated sheet. They're raised on sheet farms, slaughtered, and taxidermied. The sheets you buy at the store are ghost corpses.

And it's all fun and games until the image of dental veneers pops into her head again. White, white pseudo-teeth. So wrong. She dreams they sink into her neck.

Waking again, it's mid-afternoon. The air conditioner has quit entirely. The oxygen in the room has died from exhaustion. Or, so it seems. And yet she doesn't mind. Well, she does mind. But she doesn't mind as much as she would if she were in a different *frame of mind*. She finds herself giving in to the heat.

She imagines the blankets are strata of soil. She imagines she's baking under six feet of dry, cracked earth. She imagines the breathlessness of it all, the dreamlessness of it all. It sounds both comfortable and sad. Do corpses grieve for themselves? Do they mourn the fact they can no longer dream (or daydream)?

Her phone rings. Or rather, it beeps. Kaye pretends it's the sound of a backhoe going in reverse. It's there to pile more dirt onto her grave. They want to make certain she can't escape. Her phone beeps again. Or rather, this time, bloops (a bloop is a bleep with a deeper tone). This means someone has left a message via ouija board. They want to summon her, but she refuses all commerce with necromancers.

Now, the cordless landline rings. The necromancers refuse to be ignored. Charlie picks it up. She hears him chattering away in the kitchen. He knocks on the door, but doesn't wait for permission to open it. His face appears in the threshold.

"Honey," he says, "Anne Owling passed away. Her niece wants to know if the church is available for a funeral on Saturday."

The news stirs her awake (horribly, irrevocably awake). It makes her ashamed of having spent the whole day in her head. She's a priest. Her congregation needs her. She hears her mother's voice: "Congregations deserve the composure and dignity of a man."

The Role

Kaye is a hot mess. She knows this.

St. Luke's doesn't need a hot mess. It needs someone confident in their orthodoxy. It needs someone tirelessly genteel. The Owling family doesn't need a hot mess. They need the comfort that only a good priest can provide.

Can Kaye be a good priest?

Well, she might be able to fake it.

Can Kaye be a sane priest?

She might be able to fake that, too.

It won't be that hard. I'll just pretend I'm an actress in some prestige TV drama about a female Episcopal priest. Yes, that's what I'll do. It sounds kind of fucked up, but it's not, really. When one becomes a priest, one makes an implicit (but binding) agreement to "act like a priest". Sometimes, the role comes naturally. Other times, one must resort to affectation. Priesthood is a daily bill that must be paid.

"Honey? Did you hear me?"

"Huh?"

Charlie points to their cordless landline phone. "Anne Owling's niece."

"Oh yes, tell her that shouldn't be a problem."

"But the Diocese, the Regathering Pl…"

"Well, I'm sure they don't expect us to park her casket in the courtyard and do it there. The Bishop will understand."

"Yeah, but…"

"It's an Owling!"

"You shouldn't give her an answer until you've cleared it."

"Give me the phone!"

Charlie keeps it. Stammers into the receiver. "S-she said yes." Then he hangs up. Glares at her. "You didn't have to yell."

Kaye rolls her eyes. "You haven't *begun* to hear me yell!"

That's the kind of thing her mother would say. She prays Charlie doesn't take note of this and point it out. Thankfully, he's out the door before he can think of it. She's alone now. She feels safe again.

The demands of practicality have pulled her up from the gutter of half-dreams and half-day dreams. She rises, aching. Hums one of her favorite hymns. Marches to the bathroom.

It takes a while for the shower to warm up. The water comes out frigid and wounding, a volley of liquid darts. She loses her footing. A drowned worm has somehow found its way into the shower. She slips on its corpse. Falls backwards. Lands with a resounding thud. Hits the back of her head on the shower wall. Her scalp stings. A knot rises. Her soul feels poisoned. No amount of water can decontaminate it.

A muffled high-pitched, squeaky, male voice calls out to her from inside the drywall. "Mental gymnastics result in mental injuries!"

Charlie pounds on the door. "Hey, what's wrong?"

"Nothing!" she screams. (A lie, of course. The honest answer is that *everything's* wrong.)

She shouldn't be living in Owlingsville. No outsider should live in Owlingsville. She is the cricket team crashing a football game.

She shouldn't be a priest. Not because she's a woman, but because she isn't capable of suspending her disbelief for more than a few months at a time. Besides, she has no talent for administration. And on top of that, she's losing her mind.

She probably shouldn't be married. Her husband treats her like a child.

Maybe, just maybe, she shouldn't be *anything*. Maybe she should drop out of society. People do that.

And she realizes now that she's burning. While she was drifting off into mental masturbation, the water became scalding. She has not yet risen from her fall. She's naked, on her knees, twisting around to avoid the shower's scourge. She manages to crawl away to the other side of the shower curtain, into the realm of mist. Then she reaches her hand back in to adjust the temperature to a more moderate warmth.

She sits atop the toilet to catch her breath. She remembers the dead worm. She feels its guts still clinging to the sole of her right foot. She grabs a piece of toilet paper to wipe it off. She'll flush it when she's done.

She can't find it. The tactile sensation remains. The visual perception is gone. She slips back into the shower. Tries to wash away all that's wrong. Tries to remind herself of all the baptisms she's performed. She has sprinkled water onto innumerable infants' foreheads, traced the sign of the cross on them, and told their beaming parents that the infant was thereby "sealed by the Holy Spirit…and marked as Christ's own forever."

This shower can be a renewal of my baptism, she tells herself. *The Holy Spirit can dwell in me once again.*

She doesn't believe it, though.

Why? Is it just too corny a sentiment to accept?

No.

I mean, obviously, it *is* corny. But that's not why she rejects the notion. No, she rejects it because her brain is an ocean. Every religious idea she has is a wave that forms, crests, and crashes. Each wave is replaced by another. Some are bigger than others, but they all suffer the same fate. They're all impermanent.

Feminist Christianity was such a wave, a massive one which enveloped her time in college, seminary, and her first parish. She still believes in it, but it no longer energizes her. Quantum Crucifixion and ChristDream were others; not quite as large but still substantial. She half-believes in them, but they no longer energize her. This Shower Baptism notion is, by comparison, tiny. She stopped believing in it right after it was born in her brain. It's barely a wave at all.

The trend disturbs her. Each wave is less consequential than the one before it! But fortunately, off in the distance of her consciousness, on her brain's horizon, a huge white cap appears. It sounds like an oncoming train. It's a tidal wave. She's going to let it take her.

A Treatment for the Septic Soul

She already has a name for this fast-approaching wave: Soul Shedding. Where does the name come from? After all, there's no *book* called Soul Shedding. No TED Talk. No podcast. Well, it just comes to her. (Perhaps via divine revelation?) Here's how it works.

You see, when the panhandler poured all of his hideous nonsense into her soul it became a reservoir of toxic waste. She thought the demands of day-to-day life would clean up that waste. But when she got out of bed to engage in a normal activity (taking a shower), the toxins reappeared. (Cold, dart-like water, the voice in the drywall, the worm on her foot.) She couldn't wash them away.

When a soul is so thoroughly poisoned, it's no longer habitable. The organism must abandon it. Just as a lizard must shed its tail to escape a predator, so too must a spiritually ailing human being shed their soul if they are to continue to live.

It's counterintuitive to think in these terms. Usually we think about the *soul* leaving the *body*. But the body can also leave the soul. In the case of soul sepsis, shedding is the only option.

How is soul shedding accomplished? Well, there's no special training required. (The lizard requires no instruction in how to shed its tail. Nature has provided all the necessary reflexes.)

In fact, most people who shed their souls aren't aware of the process as it happens. They only realize it in retrospect. Mother Kaye is the exception.

This, too, is counterintuitive. We imagine the soul to be, well, a big fucking deal. We imagine that its sudden departure would be at least as jarring as the sudden departure of our intestines. But this simply isn't the case. As it turns out, you can live for many decades without one.

This is not to say that the whole thing is inconsequential. Everything feels unreal after the soul is shed. The human organism experiences life in a far more detached manner. I suppose it could be likened to an experience of dissociation. The body will move on as an empty shell, clomping about the stage of life to perform the role it has been assigned. The brain will sometimes succumb to outrageous delusions (or half-delusions) to make sense of it all.

Post-Shedding

So, she dries off with an old towel. She wraps it around herself. She goes to the wardrobe department for her costume. (Black slacks, black clergy shirt, white clerical collar, black socks, black flats.) She emerges from the bedroom and gives Charlie a peck on the cheek. "Did you happen to write down her number, honey?"

"Oh, uh, sure. It's here someplace. But are you okay?"

"Of course I'm okay. Why do you ask?"

"You were sick."

"I was just tired."

"What are you dressed up for?"

"Anne Owling's niece needs me."

"She didn't ask for you. She just wanted to know if the church was available."

"But I'm the priest. I'll be officiating the service. I'd like to call her and arrange a visit. At the very least, we need to talk about the logistics of it all. Quite likely, she'll need some pastoral care, too. Whether she knows it or not, she'll need a listening ear."

"From the way she was talking it didn't sound like they were close."

"Then she may need me even more. How odd it must be, to have the responsibility for planning a funeral for someone you're not close to."

He pauses. Paces. "Yeah, but you're sick."

"I'm not sick, I was just tired."

"And fatigue is a COVID symptom. Just sayin'."

"If I were sick, I'd stay home."

"Then stay home."

"But I wasn't sick earlier. I just…well…had a nasty flare up of arthritis."

"Oh. Why didn't you say that earlier?"

"Because I didn't want to sound like an old lady."

"Can you still smell and taste shit?"

"Huh?"

"I mean, do you have any COVID symptoms? Let's take your temperature, at least."

An inexplicable fear inflames her nerves. An outrageous delusion (or half-delusion) crashes into her brain: *If he takes my temperature, he'll find out I'm not human. I'm just an action figure, a* female priest *action figure. Without my soul, I am plastic. I am room temperature. I mustn't let him find this out.*

"No thermometers," Kaye says. She hopes that will end the conversation.

But Charlie keeps nagging.

She pretends to give in; tells him the thermometer is in one of the medicine cabinets. He scours both bathrooms and comes up empty. Mutters something about buying a new one the next time he's at Walmart.

Kaye knows the thermometer is actually in one of the junk drawers. She put it there early in the pandemic, when she took her temperature each morning.

She feels okay about telling the lie. She only did so out of necessity.

The Dialogue

Another revelation (or half-revelation) occurs to her: she has already fucked up her life as an action figure. Most action figures don't talk! Kaye knows this because Charlie collects anime figures and none of them talk. Each one is a silent schoolgirl, hidden away in his closet. (If someone from the vestry came over to chat, they might misunderstand such a collection.)

There must be a piece of her soul still clinging to her: the part responsible for spontaneous speech. (Clinging to her like the dead worm clung to her foot.) It must be shed, too, if she is to be toxin-free.

But being a silent action figure is no good; not for life as an Episcopal priest! If she were a Catholic nun, silence might be fitting. However, the demands of *her* calling are such that she must have a voice mechanism implanted somewhere within her plastic. Or, at the very least, she must constantly *imagine* that she has a voice mechanism implanted somewhere within her plastic.

She coughs, and imagines the phlegm is the last stubborn remnant of her soul being shed. Now, the soul *of her voice* is detached, too.

As a result, Kaye's conversation with Ann Owling's niece is stilted and awkward. Yes, Kaye can talk. However, talking action figures only have a handful of phrases at their disposal.

For example, Kaye finds herself limited to six:

- *I'm so sorry for your loss.*
- *Your aunt was a sweet lady.*
- *What do you want for the service?*
- *We can do that.*
- *Let us pray.*
- *Amen.*

"I'm sorry for your loss," Kaye says upon meeting the niece in the church office.

"Thank you," the niece says.

"What do you want for the service?"

"Well, she never really talked to anyone about her preferences. What do you usually do?"

"We can do that."

"Beg pardon."

"We can do that."

"You mean, you can do what you usually do? The regular Episcopal funeral service? I suppose that makes the most sense."

"We can do that."

The niece wrinkles her brow. She frowns. She knows something is wrong with Mother Kaye. Or, at least, Mother Kaye *thinks* the niece knows something is wrong with her. To break through the awkwardness, Kaye says something new.

"Your aunt was a sweet lady."

"That's a kind thing to say. So, two p.m. on Saturday? The casket right there in the church? It's confirmed?"

"We can do that."

The niece nods. "Very well then, is there anything else for us to talk about?"

"Let us pray."

"Oh, of course. That might be helpful."

Awkward silence ensues.

And continues.

The niece is waiting for the priest to say the prayer, but instead Mother Kaye just keeps staring at her like a good action figure should. Then she bows her head. "Amen," she declares.

The niece starts itching herself all over. Mother Kaye can see she's breaking out in hives. The niece is itching her neck and legs and clomping out of the office in her high heels.

Apparently, Mother Kaye has been an agent of discomfort. Her affectation has not been entirely convincing. The trick, it would seem, is to add more phrases to the audio player embedded in her plastic.

Make Believe

Kaye looks at the clock. 6:00 p.m. Maggie's gone. The priest has the office to herself, at least for a while. The vestry meeting doesn't start for another ninety minutes.

It's a relief to know she's alone. For one thing, it means no one saw the niece furiously scratching her hives on her way out. Had Maggie been at her desk, just outside Kaye's office, she would have noted that the niece looked worse when she left than when she had entered.

Mother Kaye's job is to comfort the grief-stricken, not add to their burden. She would have looked like a failure. Looking like a failure is the worst possible outcome.

Six phrases is not enough. That's the problem. That's why she failed with the niece. Somehow, she has to add new ones before the vestry meeting. So she gets down on the floor of her office. She plays a game of make believe. She's a defective action figure abandoned on the floor. The little girl who owns her has grown tired of hearing only six phrases. So she sends Kaye off to the toy company to get an upgrade.

There's an empty cardboard box sitting next to the wastebasket—the sort of box used by office supply companies to send reams of paper. Kaye crawls over to it, grabs it, lowers herself back to the ground, and places the box over her head. This is to symbolize the process of being shipped to the toy company. It occurs to her that she should probably writhe around on the floor (she's bound to get jostled during the long ride on the mail truck).

Yes, she's going nuts.

But she *has* to go nuts, in private, so she can appear normal, in public. If she doesn't get more phrases added to her voice mechanism, she will appear stilted and awkward yet again! In fact, she will have to have the entire Episcopal funeral service (*Burial of the Dead*) added, so she can say the right words Saturday afternoon.

Is she *really* going nuts, though?

She is proclaiming herself to be an action figure. So what? How is this any different from holding up a communion wafer and proclaiming it the body of Christ? Perhaps Soul Shedding is no less a sacrament.

Maybe this is what Christ really came to teach: salvation through make-believe. He pretended the bread and wine were his body and blood, and offered it to his audience during a one-act play called *The Last Supper*. Perhaps, when he said "Do this in remembrance of me," he meant "Play make-believe games in remembrance of me."

The left side of Mother Kaye's brain starts to have a conversation with the right side.

Left Brain: *Maybe I should write a book about this new interpretation. Who knows, I might be the next big thought leader in the Episcopal Church, the mother of a new theological fad! Hell, maybe this could be a bridge to a career outside of the church. I could become a self-help guru. I could be a life coach who teaches others how to become action figures, too.*

Right Brain: *We can do that.*

Left Brain: *You really think we're up to it?*

Right Brain: *Amen!*

Left Brain: *You know I've lost my grip on reality, right? Janus took it away from me.*

Right Brain: *I'm so sorry for your loss.*

Left Brain: *It's okay. It was bound to happen sooner or later.*

Right Brain: *Let us pray.*

Left Brain: *We're not going to pray for more rain, are we?*

Right Brain: *Let us pray.*

Left Brain: *Yes, of course. Sorry for the distraction. I was just making a little joke before we enter the sacred space. Rest assured, I will say this prayer with all my heart and all my soul and all my mind. Furthermore, I will say it in the dignified verbiage used in the prayer book.*

There, on the floor, with a cardboard box over her head, Mother Kaye says her prayer. Well, she doesn't *say* it, verbally. She doesn't yet have enough words to say it. She *thinks* it.

Heavenly Father, who hast given this action figure too few words with which to converse, we beseech thee, in thy mercy, to vouchsafe her safe passage to the toy factory. Grant the employees such manual dexterity as is necessary to remove the audio mechanism implanted in her plastic and replace it with an upgrade. At this time we in the Episcopal Church celebrate the season of Pentecost. Just as the Holy Spirit appeared unto the apostles on that fateful day, bearing the gift of tongues, we ask thou to multiply the vocabulary of this figure so that she might function well in her role. In thy name we pray.

Right Brain: Amen.

Kaye's back aches. She knows it's her arthritis, but she exiles this knowledge to the wasteland of her consciousness.

The ache in her back means the factory workers are replacing her audio mechanism.

Kaye's head aches. She knows this is the natural result of stress. She probably needs to eat, too. But she banishes this knowledge to a remote, fog-enshrouded island in her consciousness. Her headache means the new audio mechanism is feeding phrases into her brain. She will still be an action figure, of course. Her speech will still have a constrained, stilted quality. Her arsenal of words will remain quite limited. However, it won't be quite as noticeable as it was with Anne Owling's niece. It will seem normal-ish.

The Vestry Meeting That Wasn't a Vestry Meeting

Anne Owling is the Senior Warden of the vestry (i.e., the big cheese). She, of course, has an airtight alibi for missing the meeting.

Sam Hardy (one of the retired social workers) is the Junior Warden. Sam is a hypochondriac. Usually he's worried about contracting insect-borne diseases. He thinks mosquitoes cause lyme disease. Even the smallest bite makes him panic. Now, he thinks he might have COVID. In a few days he'll get a test result saying he doesn't. But he doesn't know that yet. He sends Kaye a text message saying he's "just not up to" meeting.

Sabrina Kincaid is a realtor. Her husband, Chris, beats her. This is not common knowledge. The husband knows to hit her where her clothes hide the marks. She was planning to attend the meeting. She was supposed to discuss the new

Sunday School curriculum but she's still walking with a limp. So, Chris commands her to bow out.

"Tell them you've got a house to show, or tell them you've become a fucking Jew, for all I care!" She sends an email to Mother Kaye, explaining that she has to work late. She bccs her husband on the email. (That way, he can see that she's not disclosing anything that would ruin his reputation as the town's foremost general practitioner.)

Andrew Carlisle is an assistant manager at the WalMart branch of Owling Bank. He has to work late tonight. A man afflicted with schizophrenia and alcoholism pedaled his bicycle into the store—right up to the bank counter—pulled a rusty steak knife out of his fanny pack, and threatened the teller with "a clobberin'" if she didn't hand over "five hunnerd (sic) dollars in unmarked bills".

Just as her shaking hands were about to fork over the cash, the proverbial "good guy with a gun" showed up. The crazy man's blood gushed all over the teller. She will have PTSD for the rest of her life.

The story will never make the national news. The *Courier*'s coverage will be limited to a brief article under the fold of the front page. It will focus on the "hero" who stopped the robbery. Upon reading the story, the local Republicans will ask this armed vigilante to consider running for County Council. One of the incumbents has his sights set on the state legislature.

Mr. Carlisle was out to lunch at the time of the shooting, so he's more *unsettled* than *traumatized*. However, there's a hell of a lot of paperwork to do after these sorts of incidents. He has to work late. He sends his regrets to Mother Kaye via text message.

Emily Mosswood is a retired kindergarten teacher who now fancies herself to be an artist. She has severe A.D.D.

Everyone knows she has severe A.D.D. She barely ever shows up to vestry meetings at all. If she does, it's never on time. In fact, she sometimes will show up on the wrong day. Mother Kaye only asked her to join the vestry because she needed seven members. She's a no show.

Gordon Blanchard is the principal of Owlingsville Middle School. He shows up for the meeting. He attends because he wants to get away from his wife. He and Kaye are the only ones in attendance.

"I know Dave Gardner isn't able to make it," Gordon says. (Dave Gardner, as you may recall, is the church treasurer.) He always makes it. He's the seventh member.

Each month he presents bulky, fastidious reports to the vestry. He seems to enjoy his role. His reports aren't just simple exercises in addition and subtraction. He uses a lot of the technical jargon of his field. ("Amortization", "depreciation", etc.) Everyone feels smarter after listening to him. "I ran into him at Weaver's yesterday. He's got some political thing going on tonight. He sends his regards."

Weaver's is Owlingsville's *upscale* liquor store. If you like to drink but don't want to rub shoulders with winos (and are willing to pay twenty percent more per bottle for the privilege) you go to Weaver's.

"It's no biggie," Mother Kaye says. "It is what it is."

These are good phrases to say. They're trite expressions, of course, but she at least sounds more natural than she did when she talked to Anne Owling's niece.

Prayer changes things.

The Thinker

For the last four days, Anne Owling has resided at Wilcox & Sons Funeral Home. There, her blood was removed. There, it was replaced with embalming fluid. There, she was dressed up in her Sunday best. There, Owlingsville's most expensive cosmetologist labored to make her dull and thinning hair look full and lustrous. St. Luke's will be the stage, but this is the dressing room.

Wilcox is to funeral homes what Weaver's is to liquor stores. It specializes in burying Owlingsville's old money, upper middle class, and professionals. Its floors are polished marble. A lackluster copy of Rodin's *The Thinker* rests on a pedestal in the antechamber.

Archie Wilcox runs the place. He acquired the sculpture at an auction in Louisville in 1987. He thinks it gives the antechamber a touch of elegance and grandeur. Despite the name Wilcox & Sons, Archie is childless. The business was founded by his great grandfather.

Archie is the last of the Wilcoxes. He has hired people from outside of the family to do most of the embalming. He dedicates himself to the business side of things. He meets with the families. He urges them to buy "sealed caskets" that "keep out the elements". Often, he does this while goofy on unprescribed Xanax.

The families notice Archie's odd demeanor, but pretend they don't. Their brains have been mauled by an encounter with the ineffable ugliness that is death. So what if the mortician is on something? They just want to leave the room, go home, and slink into bed.

Archie has never married. Archie is gay. Archie is in the closet. Or, at least, he tries to be. Technically, he's still a virgin. Twice, during trips to Mexico, he paid to watch hustlers jack each other off. That's the closest he's ever come to having sex with another person. His primary sexual outlet is masturbation.

He has a stubborn lisp. He's tried to shed it. He even traveled to Indianapolis to see a speech therapist. These efforts have only succeeded in making him more self-conscious. He's overweight. He's tried to get fit. He even joined a gym. These efforts, too, have only succeeded in making him more self-conscious. There are many hot men at the gym. He catches quick glimpses of them whenever he thinks he can get away with it.

He attends All-American Resurrection Church. Pastor Wayne Wright keeps him at arm's length, and the rest of the congregation follows suit. If Archie were not such a generous tither, Pastor Wayne might run him off entirely. But Archie gives to All-American, and gives to the local Republican party, and gives to Donald Trump. Think of these donations as indulgences (in the medieval sense). With them, Archie buys the church's grudging acceptance. In the eyes of local Republicans, they semi-absolve Archie of the sin of effeminacy.

The Lackluster Copy of Rodin's *Thinker* is doomed to spend his life ruminating on this sad spectacle. (The Lackluster Copy is sentient. *The Thinker* thinks.)

He suspects that Archie will worry himself into a massive stroke. No one but his coworkers will attend his funeral. *They'll* only show up because it will be part of their workday. More people will show up for the reading of his will.

Yes, in Owlingsville even the statues are pessimists!

I know this sounds bleak. Surely there's at least one happy person in town. Surely, there's at least one shining example of goodness. Virtue can't have fled *entirely* from its borders! Humanity is more nuanced than that.

This is a valid criticism. So I will admit that crassness doesn't rule every heart for every moment of every day. Kindness exists in Owlingsville, but it's practiced furtively, haltingly, and inconsistently.

People feel embarrassed by even *talking about* it. Owlingsville is a practical town, and kindness is perceived as impractical. If you pick up a piece of litter or put your shopping cart back in its proper corral, you're seen as a sucker.

Ah, but what about the teachers, psychologists, and social workers who gather during coffee hour at St. Luke's? Didn't I describe them earlier as "impractical do-gooders"? Well, yes. But here's their dirty little secret: they are *professional* idealists.

Now, of course, they're not in it strictly for the money. Other fields are far more lucrative. However, most of them wouldn't spend time with their clients (or anyone *remotely like* their clients) unless they were on the clock. And the sliver of do-gooders who *would* spend their off-the-clock time with their clients (or people like their clients) do so for unhealthy reasons: they lack friends, they lack lovers, and they use their clients to meet one or both of these needs.

The kindness of the helping professional is a *strategic, forced, performative* kindness available only during office hours. The most compassionate social worker in the world may treat her own husband like shit. By the end of the day, she has run out of empathy and isn't emotionally available to him. She would treat him better if he were her client.

The same could be said for the staff at Wilcox and Sons. The Lackluster Copy of Rodin's *Thinker* has seen this for himself. The staff treat the family of the departed with the utmost respect, but only because they're customers. If this strategic, forced, performative kindness is applied with skill, they can successfully upsell the grieving family.

But what about all the people who come to the funeral to pay their respects to widows and orphans? Aren't their motives pure?

Rarely.

The Lackluster Copy has overheard many conversations during his thirty plus years in the antechamber. He knows people come to funerals to see and be seen. He knows they come to satiate their morbid interest in the condition of the corpse. He knows they come to avoid the guilt that would descend on them if they didn't come. He knows they take drugs in the bathroom to numb out. It's impossible to be kind if you're not really there.

Three Ways of Looking at Anne Owling's Funeral

Ordinarily, Archie Wilcox wouldn't be driving the hearse. But this is no ordinary occasion. Anne Owling is town royalty. He wants to be conspicuously present at the service. If people notice his involvement, it will reinforce the Wilcox & Sons brand as the town's *luxury* funeral home.

He pulls out all the stops. Wears his finest suit, white gloves, and gold cufflinks. Unfortunately, his suit is covered up by his black raincoat. It started pouring at six a.m. and it shows no sign of letting up. It's odd to get this much rain in June. Odder still to have to navigate flash flooding on Church Street. Owlingsville is unaccustomed to such occurrences. Even the conservative editorial page of the *Courier* mentioned the need for an overhaul of the gutters and drainage system downtown, as they aren't fit for "the new era of climate change".

Archie thinks climate change isn't real. Or, at least, he hopes it's not real. He'd hate to have to cover up his suit with a raincoat all the time. (Archie hates his raincoat. It's not as snazzy as his suit. He bought the raincoat at the Dillard's up in Bloomington. He usually only shops at the Neiman Marcus in Indianapolis.)

Speaking of Indianapolis, that's where he had to go to rent the Rolls Royce hearse he's using for the occasion. He's not charging the Owling family extra for this. He sees Anne Owling's funeral as a loss leader. Every well-to-do future corpse in town will be at the service. He wants them to think he's good enough to serve them, too.

It's been at least fifteen years since he's been inside St. Luke's. The last time was for the funeral of Anne's husband, Jack Owling. Some of Jack's old cronies at Owling Resources had asked Anne's permission to place a pickaxe in his hands "so he can keep on minin' in Heaven". Jack had never used a pickaxe in his life. Moreover, pickaxes weren't a significant mining tool at the time of Jack's death. But Anne granted the request, so Archie made it happen.

Archie chooses his pew carefully. At first he's tempted to sit near the front, maybe even right in back of the Owlings. But then he reconsiders, opts for the *rearmost* pew. That way, when it comes time for him to supervise the pallbearers' removal of the casket, he will have to walk the entire length of the aisle to get there. Everyone's eyes will be on him. He'll feel like a bride marching up to the altar!

And yet, nobody will know he planned it out this way. In fact, they'll assume he was effacing himself and his role in the service by sitting in the back. It was only by *necessity* that he walked up to the front to do his job at the end.

He's not wearing a mask. Very few people are. No one is making a big deal out of it, either. He'd heard the Episcopals were all left wingers, so this surprises him. He'd had one prepared for the occasion. It's in his suit pocket. It's black and embossed with the Wilcox & Sons logo. He figured that way, even if he had to have his face covered, people would be able to tell who was running the show. Thankfully, it isn't needed.

These are the thoughts churning through Archie's head as the service starts. The lady pastor (as Archie thinks of her) can barely be heard this far back. She isn't mumbling. She isn't wearing a mask. But she's not projecting her voice, either.

She's holding a book in her hand but she doesn't seem to be reading out of it. It seems more like a prop. It's like she knows the service by heart. She's reciting it, the way kids in school used to have to memorize and recite "To Be or Not to Be".

All the language is old fashioned. "Thees" and "Thys" and "Thines". "For none of us liveth to himself, and no man dieth to himself," she says. Archie doesn't quite buy what she's selling. He has "liveth" to himself all his life. His only friends are corpses and coworkers. The Republicans only want him for his money. The Lackluster Copy of Rodin's *The Thinker* is a good listener, but can't ask him how he spent his weekend.

Every day he spends in Owlingsville, Archie liveth to himself and dieth to himself. He even dieth *le petit mort* by himself.

But now the pastor is already on to the next page of her book. She's praying to God, asking Him to grant Anne "an entrance into the land of light and joy". And at that exact moment rain slaps St. Luke's two hundred year old windows with disconcerting ferocity. It now looks like night out there, but it isn't night.

And Archie dreads the burial, because rain makes everything a headache. And he worries there might end up being a tornado. But the pastor (as Archie thinks of her) is fearless. She's declaring "the darkness is no darkness in thee, but the night is as clear as day; the darkness and light to thee are both alike."

And that's when the door cracks open. The click of the nob echoes through the church. A stranger walks in. He's wearing a trash bag as a makeshift raincoat, ragged pants, and hole-ridden sneakers. He's gazing at Mother Kaye and shaking his head. He seems to be exasperated by what he sees. He looks like he knows her, and he's disappointed in her.

He remains standing at the back of the church, right smack dab in the middle of the aisle, shaking his head and muttering to himself. "Rejected..." is the only word bystanders can clearly make out.

Chris Kincaid is staring at Archie and clearing his throat. The message couldn't be any clearer if it were communicated by telepathy. *You're the funeral director.* Direct *this bum out of here!* Sabrina Kincaid sees her husband staring and clearing his throat so she starts doing the same thing. Archie knows he has no choice. He sighs and approaches the stranger. "Sir, I'm afraid we're having a private function right now. Do you need the pastor for something?"

"I need the *priest*," he replies.

"Then why don't you go and wait outside. After the funeral, I'll pass on the message that someone wants to meet her. Go on now." Archie waves his hands. "Go on out."

"I am the *Ruler* of Doorways," he says. "I come and go as I please."

CHARLIE DRIVES SEPARATELY. KAYE HAS TO GET TO CHURCH early, after all. He doesn't want to sit in a pew for forty-five minutes making small talk with the organist. All she ever does is regale him with tales of her hip replacement.

Charlie hates St. Luke's. Charlie hates funerals.

So, for Charlie, a funeral *at* St. Luke's is a double dose of annoyance. Of course, no one *loves* funerals. At least, no one *besides funeral directors*. But most of us can find a way to tolerate them. Charlie cannot.

He finds the sight of an embalmed corpse unbearably depressing and unnatural. The people who dress up *to gawk at* that corpse strike him as equally depressing and unnatural. *Their souls are long dead and mummified*, he tells himself. *This church is long dead and mummified. It's dead but it doesn't know it. It's dead but it keeps on walking. This church is Boris Karloff in ragged bandages. This church is a monster. Kaye's a necromancer who gets up way too early every Sunday morning to recite the magickal incantations that keep it going. But the spell is losing its power. Each time it's cast, it yields diminishing returns.*

Charlie has, of course, cast spells before. Those are different, though. The occasional excursion to a convention notwithstanding, he is, for the most part, a solitary practitioner. Given his circumstances, he has to be. But there's *freedom* in solitude. He need not kowtow to any particular tradition. He can pick and choose ingredients from the cornucopia of world history.

My spirituality is a fusion cuisine, he thinks. *A little bit Mediterranean (working with Pan), a little bit Native American (the sweat lodges), a little bit Asian (the occasional round of Zen meditation), and a little bit Anglo-American (interests in ghost hunting and Wicca).*

*No one else in this congregation even knows what "fusion cuisine"
is! Not even in the literal sense. They definitely couldn't wrap their heads
around applying it figuratively to a type of spirituality.*

Yes, Charlie finds it helpful to remind himself that he's
smarter than the people around him. His isolation seems
more natural, under such circumstances. It hurts less.

As usual, he grabs a seat in the middle of the church, on
the right hand side. He's found this to be the most tolerable
perch from which to view his wife at work. If he sits in
the back, there's gossip about how he rushes out without
even saying hello to people. If he sits in the front, he has
to endure a half-dozen mind-numbing conversations before
he makes his way outside. Old men chatting him up about
lawn maintenance and roof repair. Old women eager to talk
to him about their favorite British crime dramas. If he sits
in the middle and walks semi-speedily toward the exit, he
only has to endure two or three such conversations. He can
do that.

At least, *every other week* he can do that.

Kaye starts the service by reading platitudes from her
prayer book. The Church has two versions of each service.
Rite I has all the old fashioned language. All the scripture
quotes are from the King James edition. Rite II uses modern
language. She's using Rite I. This makes sense. Anne Owling
was ferociously uptight.

"'...though this body be destroyed, yet shall I see God...'"
Kaye says.

Actually, she isn't reading it. She's reciting it. The prayer
book is open, but she isn't looking at it. Why is she reciting
it? To prove something to herself? It doesn't sound good.
She doesn't sound like she's *really there*. She seems to be going
through the motions. The church is a machine and she's just
one of its gears.

Is he the only one who notices? He glances around to see if there's any nervous fidgeting in the congregation. He looks for raised eyebrows, too.

All of this has to be done surreptitiously. If he glances back at the congregation someone will *notice* him glancing. Then they'll be distracted from the service. *They'll* start to glance around, to see what Charlie's glancing at. And then someone else will notice *that* person glancing around, and *they'll* start glancing around.

So he pretends he has a sore back. Makes a show out of stretching to the right and the left. Works backward glances into his stretching.

He doesn't seem to notice anyone else disturbed by what they're hearing. They don't notice what he notices. Maybe the old coots have trouble hearing, so the robotic delivery doesn't faze them.

But Charlie is young. Charlie can hear. Charlie knows Kaye well enough to sense when something isn't right. *Maybe she got COVID and it's making her loopy*, he thinks. He kicks himself for forgetting to pick up a new thermometer.

"'Blessed are the dead who die in the Lord,'" Kaye says, "'...even so saith the Spirit, for they rest from their labors.'"

She needs a rest from her labors. In August they're supposed to spend two weeks in a cabin up at Pokagon State Park. But they really need to book a trip farther away, to New York or Los Angeles. Someplace where they can get lost in the crowds.

He's stirred out of these ruminations by the weather. Damn, it's so nasty out there! Of course, it was nasty on the drive over, too. But it seems to have just gotten worse. The wind and the rain is rattling the windows now. Was that hail, or just hard rain?

He looks outside. The sky's all fucked up. That's the way he thinks of it. It's broken. Malfunctioning. The wind broke the machinery of the sky. The gears and springs that run daytime mode got blown off. So the machine defaulted to night mode.

He doesn't really believe that, of course. The machinery idea is just a metaphor. But then again, many of his spiritual beliefs are just metaphors. Does he *really* believe in Pan? Or, is Pan just a symbol of his id? Sometimes he thinks of his paganism as a live action role playing game. Yes, that's what it is. A LARP designed by Carl Jung, which allows him to express important aspects of his psyche, of his *humanity*.

Sometimes, when he's making love to Kaye he isn't really *making love* to Kaye. He's *fucking* her, hard and fast. He's *having* her. *Using* her. That's when his body is possessed by Pan's spirit. Pan delights in seducing a priest. It's the closest he will ever get to defiling Christ, Himself.

But is Pan really possessing Charlie? Or is Charlie merely *imagining* this? Does such an act of the imagination help him vent his resentment against Christianity; resentment he can't speak aloud for fear of upsetting Kaye?

What difference does it make if it is "only" his imagination. One of his favorite speakers, a statuesque witch up in Fort Wayne, is fond of saying "...you can't spell 'imagination' without 'magi'". The imagination is a magickal faculty, capable of inducing changes in consciousness.

These are the sorts of thoughts sailing through Charlie's head during the funeral. I believe they demonstrate that his beliefs are almost as shaky as Kaye's. He, too, must perform mental gymnastics to keep them going.

Charlie's *beliefs* are unstable, just like Kaye's. But his *behavior* is stable, unlike hers. That is the difference between them.

And why is his behavior stable? Because his beliefs are less central to his identity than Kaye's are to hers? Possibly. Kaye occupies a public role in Christianity. I suppose you could call her a *professional* Christian. And, as I've reminded you many times, she wants to keep her job.

Charlie, on the other hand, occupies a private, closeted role in pagan circles. This enables him to tinker with his beliefs with little risk of public scrutiny or financial ruin. There is, in one sense, less pressure on him. That explains why he's less erratic.

Or does it?

The closet is far from a comfortable place. It's suffocating. It's ruled by fear. It's, well, *inconvenient*. He has to drive hours away from Owlingsville to hang out with his tribe! Kaye never joins him, not even as a supportive bystander.

There must be another explanation for his relative stability. Here's one possibility: Charlie's behavior is less erratic because he has never seen what Kaye saw. He wasn't in that pavilion with the panhandler who wasn't a panhandler. He didn't hear Janus's confession. He had no Toxic Mystery poured into his soul, therefore his body had no need to evacuate.

But then he hears a clicking sound, followed by the sound of the front door's ancient knob turning. And he sees a man come in and loiter at the back. He sees him looking up at Kaye and shaking his head.

To Archie, Chris, and Sabrina, the stranger looked like a bum. That's pretty much what Kaye saw in the park, too. That's what almost everyone who looks at the stranger sees.

Charlie is the only one in Owlingsville who sees him as a set of conjoined twins joined at the vertebrae, back to back. At least, that's the way his brain initially tries to make sense of what he sees. Eventually, he realizes that the Mystery is, in fact, a single entity. He just happens to have two faces. A smooth, young face gazes at the altar. A bearded, wrinkled face looks towards the exit.

Charlie is the only one who sees Janus in his true form, but the name Janus doesn't occur to him at the time. This is the hazard of the cafeteria approach to spirituality. Charlie knows everything about Pan, but nothing about the pantheon. There's a thin line, perhaps, between fusion and confusion.

That's not real, he thinks.

But is it really a *thought*? A declaration? No, it's more like a *prayer*. A supplication. He's praying for it not to be real.

Praying to what, though?

To reason? To reality? To science? Normality? Yes, I suppose that's the best way of putting it. He's praying to each. If he were still in possession of his senses, he might express his thought as a conscious prayer to Athena, the goddess of reason. But what would such a prayer accomplish? It would be an absurd action! Prayer is an inherently irrational act, a sort of *dream* action taken when the analytical mind is powerless to comprehend its surroundings. A goddess of reason is an oxymoron.

"I AM THE RESURRECTION AND THE LIFE," MOTHER KAYE SAYS.

Those are the first words of *The Burial of the Dead: Rite One*. She says these words in as flat and mechanical a manner as possible, but she allows herself to feel their poignancy. Turning into an action figure has, indeed, been a kind of resurrection for her. It has offered her a new, more satisfactory life. Others should follow her path.

Perhaps that's her mission in life: she is to preach The Plastic Gospel. She is to baptize followers via full immersion in cardboard (to simulate their shipment to and from the toy factory). Perhaps she should even begin wearing pink PVC or latex costumes, to make her flesh seem more convincingly plastic. Perhaps she should wear a plastic mask over her face. Perhaps that is the way to advance in holiness, in the new religion of Plastianity. The longer you stay involved with it, the more plastic you become. Highly revered figures in the movement would have their limbs amputated so they could be replaced with prostheses.

Anne Owling's casket rests a half dozen feet away from her, at the foot of the altar. She looks more plastic than she has ever appeared before, more *like an action figure* than she ever has before. Embalming does this. Mother Kaye decides that in Plastianity, cremation will be forbidden. Embalming will be elevated to a sacrament. After all, the Episcopal catechism defines a sacrament as "an outward and visible sign of an inward and spiritual grace". What greater grace can there be than the conversion of painful flesh into painless plastic?

And she continues to recite *Burial of the Dead*, of course, because that's what the voice mechanism in her back has been programmed to do under these circumstances. But within the confines of her plastic brain, she's receiving a revelation. She now knows, without a doubt, that Heaven is not an enjoyable family picnic. Heaven is an infinite toy chest filled with dolls and action figures. Plastic heads shed no tears.

She's justifiably proud to be the recipient of this revelation. And she will be the one to write all of it down in a new gospel! (Assuming the Great Molder in the Sky does not deem it sinful for an action figure to write a book. And that is a big assumption. An action figure must remain passive.)

So, it won't be *her* writing the book. She will merely be a tool used by the Great Plastic Molder to write the book.

Afterwards, the Second Person of the Plastic Trinity, the Little Boy in the Sky, will grab a hold of Mother Kaye and play with her. He will have a Mother Kaye's Office Playset, and He will move her around to simulate the typing of a manuscript.

Yes, that makes sense, too. We exist as action figures in the collection of the Little Boy in the Sky. This is why our lives seem to make so little sense. Little boys are always changing the logic of the games they play with action figures. The stories never remain consistent. One moment, Snake Eyes is beating up Cobra Commander, the next moment Han Solo shows up and recruits Snake Eyes to help destroy the Death Star. Then He-Man arrives and beats up Cobra Commander. Then Megatron shows up and blasts He-Man into dust. Then Cobra Commander turns on Megatron.

So it is with us and our jumble of shifting alliances and adversaries, the intrusion of figures from one fandom (reality television) into another (politics). This nonsense is Holy Nonsense, because it is being perpetrated by the Little Boy in the Sky.

And all the while she continues reciting *Burial of the Dead*. Perhaps this is the reason that she, unlike the others, doesn't notice the hard slapping of rain against the window, or the ghastly midday darkness, or the sudden intrusion of the Toxic Mystery into St. Luke's.

No, the first thing Mother Kaye notices is a tap on the shoulder. She's facing the congregation at the time, reciting the service. It's not the best time to turn around. But the tapper won't take no for an answer. He taps and taps and taps her shoulder, five, six, seven times. She only gives in when the tapping turns to slapping. Yes, she feels an open hand assault the crown of her head. (A head already sore and lumpy from her fall.) So, she turns around.

A lifesize plastic replica of Father Abbott stands facing her. Or is it simply Father Abbott as he appeared when he was freshly embalmed? No, it's the former. She realizes that when it retracts its molded plastic finger from her shoulder. The likeness is impeccable: the skinny, bespectacled, half-bald old man in clerical garb.

A voice emits from a speaker in his chest. "You're under a lot of strain. Why don't you go spend time with your friend? I can take over the funeral for you. I mean, the family would actually appreciate it. Anne and I saw eye-to-eye on so many things."

And she realizes that Father Abbott is more plastic than she is. She still looks human. He looks truly artificial. According to the dictates of Plastianity, that makes him her superior. She realizes he's not so much making a request as issuing an order. She obeys, because she believes.

The congregation gasps as Mother Kaye abandons her post at the altar, passes to the side of Anne Owling's casket, and calls out to the man standing at the door. (The man she hadn't noticed until now. Her friend.) "I'm coming," she cries.

Dave Garland looks like he wants to tackle her before she leaves. He doesn't, because that would be gauche. Charlie wants to do something, but he's dazed. Chris Kincaid looks like he wants to hit her, but he never hits anyone in front of witnesses. So he just silently fumes.

She's genuinely puzzled by these reactions. Yes, it's unorthodox to leave halfway through a service, but her substitute is right there for everyone to see. "Father Abbott will take it from here," she says. Then she crosses the threshold into the howling storm.

The Gossip

By Monday afternoon, gossip about the strange occurrences at Anne Owling's funeral has spread throughout town. Nearly all of it is mistaken.

For example, Mother Kaye is once again referred to as a "nun". (Specifically, "That nun who ran off with a homeless man.") That gossip fails to impress, though. ("Who's surprised by that? She openly ran around with that school teacher. Guess she got a hankerin' for a bad boy, instead!")

Some focus their efforts on ridiculing Charlie as a cuckold. Eleanor Crosby, the retired cheerleading coach who sat next to Charlie at the funeral, obsesses on this perspective. She tells her successor (the *current* cheerleading coach at Owlingsville High School) about it over lunch at Arlen's Sandwich Shop.

"He pissed his pants, that's the God's honest truth. Can you believe it? His woman was running off with another man, practically right in front of the whole town, and what does he do? Leave his pew and fight for her? No, he pisses his pants! I don't know, maybe he was glad to be rid of her.

Like, maybe he didn't really like women! Honestly, I wouldn't be surprised if he ended up spooning with Archie Wilcox someday. He didn't seem like much of a man, to my way of lookin' at things."

Other stories allege Mother Kaye ran St. Luke's weekly soup kitchen as her own personal male brothel. "Only bums with big dicks were given a bite to eat," an old lady behind the counter at Subway tells her coworker. "She used to tell them: 'If you want somethin' in your mouth, then I gotta have somethin' in mine!'"

St. Luke's doesn't even operate a soup kitchen.

THERE ARE TWO REASONS CHARLIE CAN'T FILE A MISSING person's report.

First of all, nearly all the witnesses perceived her departure as a deliberate act, freely chosen. And, honestly, who's to say they weren't right? Maybe her failure to resign her priesthood was a decision. Maybe she *wanted* the burden of unreality.

Second (and perhaps more importantly), she's not actually missing. People report seeing her all the time! She has become strangely ubiquitous. Most people, in fact, do not go a single day without seeing her. But everyone sees her, well, *differently*.

"I saw that mad nun hitchhikin' out on the county road Saturday night. She was wearin' short shorts like some kinda whore!"

"I saw her picking trash out of a barrel at the Little League field. She was wearing a sundress."

"Nah, she has a regular job now. She's workin' in the garden department at WalMart."

"Nope. She's a librarian now. Saw her teaching an old lady how to add a .gif to her tweets."

"She's an orderly at the state hospital."

"Orderly? She's a patient!"

"Patient? She works in the cafeteria!"

"Lunch lady? Nah, she's a prison guard."

Some people are starting to see her multiple times the same day. In the morning, she'll appear to them as a crossing guard outside Owlingsville Elementary. At lunch, she'll be their waitress. At dinner, she'll be the newscaster reading off a teleprompter.

The Little Boy in the Sky delights in playing with her, you see. He's forever casting her in new roles, changing the digital files in her voice pack, putting her in new outfits.

It's enough to make Charlie a recluse. He refuses to turn on a television or walk outdoors, as he knows he'll encounter her (in some incarnation or another). She has become hideously mutable.

Some people see two versions of her at the same time, only twenty feet apart. They have no vocabulary for this. (The word "bilocation" never comes to mind.) The Great Molder delights in making more copies of her, you see. His little boy is demanding, and wants as many copies as possible.

Fortunately, little boys eventually grow tired of their toys. Someday soon, the sightings will end abruptly. But in the meantime, Owlingsville is haunted in a most unusual way and everyone is anxious to start their summer vacations.

About the Author

NICOLE CUSHING IS A BRAM STOKER AWARD® WINNING novelist and a two-time nominee for the Shirley Jackson Award. Various reviewers have described her work as "cerebral", "brutal", "transgressive", "wickedly funny", "taboo", "groundbreaking" and "mind-bending".

Her second novel, A Sick Gray Laugh (2019) was named to LitReactor's Best Horror Novels of the Last Decade list and the Locus Recommended Reading List. Her third novel, Mothwoman was released in late 2022. Cemetery Dance Publications will be releasing Nicole's next novella, The Plastic Priest, in paperback and ebook editions in late 2023.

Nicole lives in Indiana.

CEMETERY DANCE
PUBLICATIONS

We hope you enjoyed your
Cemetery Dance Paperback!
Share pictures of them online, and tag us!

Instagram: @cemeterydancepub
Twitter: @CemeteryEbook
TikTok: @cemeterydancepub
www.facebook.com/CDebookpaperbacks

Use the following tags!

#horrorbook #horror #horrorbooks
#bookstagram #horrorbookstagram
#horrorpaperbacks #horrorreads
#bookstagrammer #horrorcommunity
#cemeterydancepublications

SHARE THE HORROR!

BITTERS,
by Kaaron Warren

The giant metal man has stood for hundreds of
years, head tilted back, mouth open. All the dead
of the town are disposed of this way, carried up
the long, staircase that winds around him and
tipped in...

McNubbin is a happy man with all he wants in
life. He's carried the bodies up since he was 14,
a worthwhile, respected job. But when he notices
broken girl after broken girl, he can't stay quiet,
and speaking up will change his perfect life.

*"A must-read for fans of menacing, thought-provoking,
horror-laced dystopias."*

—Library Journal

Made in the USA
Middletown, DE
05 December 2023

43372358R00066